Retribution

Chet Hallam stayed in Texas when his family moved to Kansas. Five years passed before he paid them a visit and, when he reached Spruce Bend, bad news awaited him. His father, the county sheriff, had left town one morning and never returned. Chet set out to find him, but local trouble intervened, took up his attention and his time. Resolute, he faced flying lead, fought back with no regard for his own life, and slowly gained the initiative from a criminal element. Arnie, his stepbrother, was an enigma, and Maisie, a saloon girl, whom Chet had known in Texas, added to his problems, until a gun showdown blasted away the opposition and he went on to discover the truth about his missing father. . . .

Retribution

Corba Sunman

A Black Horse Western

ROBERT HALE

© Corba Sunman 2016
First published in Great Britain 2016

ISBN 978-0-7198-2057-1

The Crowood Press
The Stable Block
Crowood Lane
Ramsbury
Marlborough
Wiltshire SN8 2HR

www.crowood.com

Robert Hale is an imprint
of The Crowood Press

Typeset by
Derek Doyle & Associates, Shaw Heath
Printed and bound in Great Britain by
CPI Group (UK) Ltd, Croydon, CR0 4YY

ONE

Chet Hallam reined in when he saw the lights of Spruce Bend, Kansas. He was tall in the saddle; twenty-five years old, a handsome man with the vitality of youth. He was wearing a store suit. A .45 pistol was holstered on his right thigh. His pale eyes were shaded by a black Stetson. He sighed as bad thoughts of his past surged through his mind, but he was happy now because at last he would see his father again. He touched spurs to his dun, and the tired horse, sensing stable and food near at hand, went forward eagerly. Chet slumped in his saddle. He had ridden up from Texas, where he had been a Texas Ranger for five years. The last letter he had received from his father, Sheriff Arch Hallam, had not been written in the old man's natural optimistic style and, reading between the lines, Chet had turned in his Ranger badge and set out to see his father – their first meeting in five long years.

He had never been to Kansas before. His father had quit Texas and moved north to find a new life, taking his wife and Chet's half-brother, Arnie Mayhew, with him. Thinking of Arnie, three years his senior, Chet was filled with all the old hatreds that had gripped him before he was left alone in Texas. Arnie had not been easy to live with, and Chet was reluctant to renew his association with his half-kin whose father had been an outlaw.

When he reached Spruce Bend he rode into the stable. A lantern was casting dim yellow light and heavy shadows through the interior. There was no sign of the stableman. Chet unsaddled the dun, threw a forkful of sweet-smelling hay into the manger, and added a scoop of crushed oats from a nearby barrel. He slung his saddlebags over his left shoulder, took his rifle in his right hand, and left the stable, eager to get his first sight of the town. He was in the doorway when a harsh voice growled from the shadows inside the stable.

'Hold it, Bucko. Stand still and don't move your hands.'

Chet obeyed, standing very still. 'Who are you?' he countered. 'I'm a stranger here – just rode in. What do you want? Is this a hold-up?'

'I'm the local deputy sheriff – Sol Kennedy, watching for undesirables. How come you waited until sundown before riding into town? What have you got to hide? What's the attraction here that's bringing a string of you long riders this way? You got a lot to answer for, mister.'

'I've ridden a far piece over the past weeks, and didn't loiter on the way. I've just taken care of my horse and now I want to get some grub and a drink. Come along and I'll buy you a beer, but don't hold me up here.'

'Don't get smart, buster.' Kennedy was a powerful man, tall and broad-shouldered. His face was shadowed by the brim of his Stetson. 'What's your name? State your business in town. We've got too many hard cases around here, and I'm cracking down on your kind.'

'I don't know what you think I am, but my father is the local sheriff, Arch Hallam, and I've come up from Texas to see him. I'm Chet Hallam.'

'Hallam! Yeah, we had a sheriff named Hallam, but he rode out four weeks ago without a word to anyone, leaving his wife and a son behind, and he ain't been seen since. Local talk is that he threw in with the outlaws hereabouts, and he'll be arrested if he shows up again. OK, I'll take what you say as the truth, so get out of here. I'll check on you tomorrow.'

'Tell me where I can find my mother,' Chet said. 'I need to see her now.'

'Mrs Hallam? She's living in a shack at the far end of town. There are three rows of shacks down there where the sidewalk ends. She's in the first row, third along. You better watch your step around town. There are some folks who don't take kindly to being fooled, especially by a lawman being paid to take care of them. I reckon that was why Hallam took off – there was talk of a lynching if he's ever caught.'

Chet moved out, his mind frozen with shock. What had been going on around here? His father was the

7

straightest man he had ever known! He went along the sidewalk, his brain buzzing as he kept to the shadows close to the buildings. He passed a saloon, heard the sounds of music and revelry inside, but resisted the temptation to take a look. As he passed an alley mouth beside the saloon he heard a woman's voice from the shadows within, and a man's voice in quick reply, telling her to remain silent. Chet peered into the alley, and saw two figures silhouetted by lamplight issuing from a side window just beyond them.

The man, big, burly and powerful, was holding the woman by her shoulder. His face was in shadow, and when he sensed Chet's presence he growled a stark message.

'Get the hell outa here, mister, or I'll gut-shoot you.'

Chet was only a couple of feet from the pair, and the warning sent him into action without hesitation. He thrust his right hand forward and the muzzle of his Winchester jabbed sharply into the man's stomach, eliciting a harsh curse. He caught the quick motion of a hand dropping to a holster and didn't waste time. He lifted his left hand to the rifle for a two-handed grip and swung it in a fast arc, delivering the butt against the man's jaw. There was a clopping sound at the contact and the man spun away; dropped to the ground.

Chet stepped forward a short pace and kicked with his right foot, his boot taking the man cleanly on the jaw. The man subsided without a sound. The girl, just a shadow with the light behind her, came forward. She was gasping for breath. Her face showed up pale as she emerged into the uncertain light on the street.

'Thank you,' she said hurriedly. 'He dragged me in there off the sidewalk – asked for money.'

'Glad to have been of help, ma'am,' Chet responded, peering closely at her. Despite the uncertain light he could see she was young, probably about twenty-five, and she was a good-looker, he could tell, although unable to see much of her face. 'This sounds like a rough town,' he observed, 'and you shouldn't be out alone after dark.'

'I was visiting a friend. I'm Lucy Johnson. My father owns the general store. He usually fetches me, but he's not feeling well tonight.'

'We haven't passed the store,' he observed. 'I'll see you home, but you should report this incident to the sheriff's office.'

'No,' she said emphatically. 'I won't do that – it's a bad idea. Thank you for helping me. You're a stranger in town.' She changed the subject adroitly.

'I just rode in,' he replied as they walked along the boardwalk.

'Are you planning on staying around?'

'I don't rightly know at the moment. I'm here to visit my family. I haven't seen them in five years.'

They reached the door of the general store. Lights were showing inside, although the door was locked. Lucy produced a key and inserted it into the lock.

'Thank you again for coming to my rescue,' she said. 'You must call in tomorrow and see my father.

9

He'll want to thank you personally.'

'It was my pleasure, Miss.' Chet touched the brim of his Stetson and waited until she had entered the store. When he heard the key turn in the lock he went on along the sidewalk.

He walked the length of the street, saw the shacks the deputy had mentioned, and counted them as he passed along the first row. There was lamplight showing at the window of the third shack. He knocked on the door with the butt of his rifle, saw a shadow inside pass between the lamp and the window, and then a voice which he recognized as his mother's called out, demanding his identity.

'It's Chet, Ma,' he replied, unaccustomed emotion catching at his throat, making his voice husky.

The door was unbarred and swung open. His mother stepped into the doorway. His face was illuminated by the light inside the room, and she uttered a cry of delight as she saw him – enveloped him with her arms. She was laughing and crying as she kissed him. Chet hugged her, but called a halt to her welcome.

'We'd better get inside out of the light,' he said. 'I'm making a big target, standing here with my back to the shadows.'

She grasped his arm to pull him inside the shack but a harsh voice cut at them.

'Hold it right where you are, Hallam, and don't try anything. Turn around and stand still.'

Chet pushed his mother into the shack, closed the door, and then turned to face the challenge. He saw

10

a law star glinting on the shirt front of the big man who came out of the shadows, a gun levelled in his hand. He suppressed a sigh when he recognized Sol Kennedy.

'It didn't take you long to find trouble, huh?' Kennedy demanded. 'I thought I'd have trouble from you. Why did you hit Joe Hoyt? You broke his jaw.'

Chet explained the incident that had occurred in the alley.

'The hell you say!' Kennedy shook his head. 'Hoyt tells it differently – says you got the drop on him and demanded money; hit him with your rifle when he tried to resist.'

'I've got a witness who will tell it as it happened, which is not how Hoyt told it. Who is Hoyt, anyway?'

'He's the banker's son. John Hoyt is a big man around here. You made a mistake tangling with his son. John Hoyt and Judge Wilson are mighty close. In fact, the judge is a friendly man, unless he's sitting in his courtroom. Come on. I'm taking you in.'

'You'd better check on my witness before you think of arresting me,' Chet protested.

'There's no need for that. Joe Hoyt made a complaint, and I'm arresting you.'

'Wait until I've told my mother where I'm going.' Chet turned and opened the door of the shack. His mother was standing by the table, one hand to her mouth.

'I won't be long, Ma,' he said. 'I'm going along to the law office to sort out a misunderstanding.'

11

She nodded mutely, and Chet departed. As he closed the door he felt a hand snatch his pistol out of its holster, and whirled to face the deputy. Kennedy was grinning.

'Just a precaution,' he said. 'You might be tempted to try something foolish, and then I'd have to shoot you. Do you know where the jail is?'

'I didn't see it on the way in because of the trouble I had. Tell me which way to head.'

'Make for that alley where you hit Joe Hoyt. Then cross the street and you'll walk into the law office opposite. Hand over your rifle. You can have your weapons back if the sheriff says so.'

Chet retraced his steps to the main street and headed for the alley beside the saloon, looking around as he did so. He saw that most of the buildings in this part of the street were in darkness, but lights blazed in a big building across the street opposite the saloon. Chet headed for it, crossing the street without being told by Kennedy, and entered the civic centre through a wide doorway. It was a brick building with a sign beside the door indicating that the law office was only a small part of the official departments inside.

'Go up the stairs at the end of the corridor,' Kennedy directed.

There were a number of closed doors on either side of the corridor, and Chet's boots echoed as he went ahead. He mounted the staircase and halted in front of a framework of solid-looking iron bars from the ceiling to the floor, blocking off the law department behind. Beyond the bars was the law office. A small man was seated at a desk set by a barred window in the back wall, and he looked up in response to Kennedy's harsh voice.

'Hey, Pete, open up, will ya? I got a customer for you.'

Pete put down the newspaper he was reading and got to his feet. He picked up a bunch of keys from the desk as he came around it, drawing a pistol and covering Chet as he unlocked the door in the bars. There was a grin of anticipation on his stubbly face as he swung the heavy door open.

'What's he done?' Pete demanded. 'Come on in, mister,' he invited with a grin. 'I'm Pete Sayer, the town jailer.' He was a lot older than Chet had thought at first sight. His sharp-featured face was lined with a network of wrinkles from chin to forehead. His eyes were blue, his straggly hair tinted with grey patches. 'Don't give me any trouble while you're in here and you might get off light. We're tough on strangers who come to town looking for trouble.'

'Save it, Pete,' Kennedy cut in. 'Is Buck in?'

'Yeah, he's in the big cell playing poker with his cronies. You ain't gonna disturb him, are you?'

'Not me. You are. Get him out here. Tell him I've got Arch Hallam's son, from Texas. He busted Joe Hoyt's jaw when they tangled in the alley beside the saloon.'

'The hell you say!' Sayer shook his head as he looked at Chet. 'You're in big trouble, Hallam. I wouldn't want to be in your boots for all the oil in

Texas. How come you tangled with Joe Hoyt? Go over to the desk and sit down on the chair in front of it. Sol, watch him while I fetch the sheriff.'

'You talk too much, Pete,' Kennedy retorted. 'Get on with it or we'll be here all night, and I got a lot of things planned for this evening.'

'So you're still after that Maisie gal in the saloon, huh?' Sayer laughed and went to a metal door in the left-hand wall, opened it, and scurried into the room beyond.

'Sit down, Hallam,' Kennedy said, 'and you better tell the truth straight off when the sheriff starts asking questions. Like I said, I got other things to do later, so don't hang me up.'

Chet sat down on the chair in front of the desk and looked around. His father had been the sheriff here for about five years, and he could not believe the old man had up and left without telling someone where he was going. He certainly would not have left his wife! Chet could only assume that his father had been killed, and his thoughts ran fast and deep. He heard voices in the room that Pete had entered, and a moment later the jailer reappeared, his face set in a harsh grimace. He closed the door with a bang and came back to the desk, still carrying his pistol.

'Buck said you must be outa your mind, disturbing him now. He said to lock Hallam in a cell and he'll get around to him later.'

'You're giving me a lot of trouble, Hallam,' Kennedy said harshly.

'It seems to me you're the one giving out a hard

time,' Chet replied. 'I haven't broken the law, and I've got a witness who can testify that I hit Hoyt while he was in the process of committing a felony. You'll think twice about putting me behind bars if you want to avoid facing a charge of wrongful arrest. I'll certainly make that charge against you if you don't turn me loose, and I'll push it to the limit. Think before you act, Kennedy.'

The deputy glanced at the big clock on the back wall and muttered under his breath. He gazed into Chet's taut face for several moments, and then glanced at the clock again.

'If the sheriff can't be bothered to handle you now then why should I?' Kennedy thrust the rifle back to Chet, who took it quickly. 'Go on and get out of here,' he snarled, handing over Chet's pistol. 'If the sheriff wants you then he'll come looking for you in the morning. Don't leave town in the meantime. You got that straight?'

'I'm not going anywhere,' Chet replied. 'I've come all the way from Texas to see my father, and I won't leave until I've found out what's happened to him.'

'Get outa here before I change my mind,' Kennedy rasped.

Chet departed quickly, and paused in the shadows on the sidewalk. He looked around the street, wondering about his father. The more he heard the less he believed. He knew his father well. He went back along the street, heading for his mother's shack, and the darkness around him seemed hostile, filled with danger.

Mrs Hallam opened the door to Chet's knock, and gazed at him in disbelief. 'Did they let you go?' she demanded.

'Why shouldn't they, Ma? I told you it was a misunderstanding. But what's happened to Pa? I heard he disappeared without warning. What's going on around here?'

'Come and sit down and I'll tell you what I know while I'm preparing a meal for you. There is bad trouble in the county, and your pa never got to grips with it. There's a gang hiding out somewhere around – and they gave Arch a lot of trouble. About two months ago some of the gang came into town to rob the bank. Your pa heard shots fired and went to investigate. He caught the gang leaving the bank and challenged them. Shooting broke out, and a small child was killed in the cross-fire – one of Pa's shots ricocheted from some metal and hit her.'

Chet shook his head. 'That was real bad,' he observed. 'I can imagine what it did to Pa.'

'He went to pieces after that, and a few weeks later he disappeared. He took his horse from the stable, told Tom Lambert, the livery man, that he was going out to try and get a line on Frazee's gang, and never came back.'

'What do you think happened to him? You lived with him, knew his every mood. And I can't believe he just rode away from here, leaving you alone and not even telling you goodbye! That's not like Pa! I hate to say it, but I've got a feeling he's dead, Ma.'

'That's what I think!' Mrs Hallam sat down at the

16

table and put her hands to her face, shoulders trembling as she wept. 'There was no one I could turn to. They brought in another sheriff, and no one has tried to find out what happened to Pa.'

'What about Arnie? Ain't he here in town with you?' He considered his half-brother, whom he had never liked. Arnie was three years older, and had never acted like he was family. He had taken an instant dislike to his stepfather; would only call him by his name, and Chet knew him as a bully, wilful and selfish.

'You know life was never good between Arnie and Arch. When we arrived here, Arnie soon went his own way. He left us, and I've only seen him half a dozen times in the last five years. He drives the local stage coach, and rarely shows up in town. Although he's my son, I know he's got some bad ways. His father was like that, and when I married your father I hoped that some of his goodness would rub off on Arnie.'

'Arnie never gave me a chance,' Chet said, shaking his head. 'But I'm here now, and I'll find out what happened to Pa.'

'I'll get you something to eat. You must be hungry.'

'No, thanks, Ma,' Chet shook his head. 'I need to take a look at the town, and I'll get some grub along the street. I'll be back later, and then we'll have a good talk about what's been happening around here.'

He placed his rifle in a corner of the room and left

17

the shack. His thoughts were grim as he went back to Main Street, his right hand close to the butt of his pistol as he headed for the saloon, attracted by the bright lights and the sound of a piano being thumped. He glanced into the alley mouth where he had hit Joe Hoyt, and questions flooded into his mind to which he could find no answers.

The batwings were in constant motion as men entered or left the saloon. Chet paused by a front window and peered through the dusty glass. There were more than twenty men inside the cigarette smoke-filled room, some standing at the long bar, the rest seated at the small tables dotted around the interior. He noted several were eating – the rest playing cards. He went to the batwings and shouldered his way into the saloon.

The noise intensified as he made his way to the bar. A 'tender, wearing a clean white apron, was busy serving customers. He was tall and heavily built, older than forty, and sweating profusely. Chet waited patiently until the man came to him with an unspoken question in his dark eyes.

'I want a meal,' he said, 'a big steak with all the trimmings; followed by apple pie.'

'See the waitress for food,' the man replied. 'If you want a beer with your meal then get it now, and take a seat over that side.' He pointed to an area on the left side of the batwings. 'Give your order to the waitress when she comes through from the kitchen. Do you want a beer?'

'Sure thing.' Chet slapped a silver coin on the bar

18

and a big glass of foaming beer was placed before him. He took it to one of the empty tables across the room and sat down.

He waited patiently for a waitress to appear, and when she did she delivered a meal to one of the waiting men and then came to Chet's table. She was a tall blonde in her twenties, neatly dressed in a black skirt, white blouse, and a frilly pink apron. She took a note pad from a pocket and produced a pencil. Chet gave his order and she nodded, writing it down, her brow furrowed.

'I'll bring it as soon as it's ready,' she said and departed quickly.

He sat drinking his beer, watching his surroundings, and stiffened when Kennedy, the deputy, came pushing through the batwings and paused on the threshold, looking around at faces. A slight hush fell over the men present, and that told Chet a great deal about Kennedy. When the deputy spotted Chet he came across the room, a slight swagger in his stride.

'I thought you'd be having a welcome home party at the shack,' he observed.

Chet ignored the observation. 'Do you want me for something?' he demanded.

'There's nothing in particular. I've dropped in to hear Maisie sing. Have you got a guilty conscience about something? You look tense, as if something is bothering you.'

Chet did not answer, and Kennedy moved away as a woman appeared at the far end of the room and paused beside a man seated at a piano. She was blonde, dressed in an elegant red dress that left her shoulders bare and exposed a great deal of her upper curves. There were whistles of appreciation from the watching men and silence came slowly in expectation of the song she was about to sing. Chet studied her face, feeling that he knew her from somewhere. She looked around thirty, and waved and called to those men she knew.

Kennedy had called her Maisie, and Chet racked his mind trying to place her until it came to him. She had been a singer in a big saloon in Kemp County, Texas, until the saloon owner was killed by the local law. He studied her more closely, nodding to himself as he recalled her. She began to sing, and he remembered the song from the old days. It had been her favourite, and his – he had been half in love with her.

Listening to the song brought back the past. She'd been caught up with the saloon owner, a bad man named Ben Travers, and Chet had killed Travers in the shoot-out that cleaned out the nest of outlaws terrorizing Kemp County. Maisie had disappeared immediately after the showdown, and Chet had often wondered what became of her. She was still doing the only job she knew, and he shook his head when he thought of what might have been between them if he had not been working for the law.

The song ended and Maisie mixed with the customers. Chet watched her intently, saw Sol Kennedy approach her, and she dismissed him summarily, her expression changing to distaste. Chet's meal arrived and he ate hungrily. He was almost through eating when Maisie reached his table.

'Hello, stranger,' she greeted, smiling. 'Are you staying long in Spruce Bend?'

'Hi, Maisie,' he replied, pushing his Stetson back off his forehead. 'How are you doing? The last time I saw you it was in Kemp County, Texas. You still can put over a song and, as I remember it, the one you just sang was our favourite. Those were the days, huh?'

She stared at him as if seeing a ghost, her expression changing quickly. But she overcame her shock and resumed smiling.

'Chet Hallam, I do declare,' she said. 'What are you doing in this part of the world? Are you still a Texas Ranger?'

He shook his head. 'I quit recently. My father was the sheriff here until he disappeared a month or so ago, and I want to discover what happened to him.'

She pulled out a chair and sat down opposite him; turned and signalled to the bar tender. Chet continued with his meal, and Maisie watched him silently until the 'tender arrived with a bottle of whiskey and two glasses.

'Are you OK, Maisie?' The 'tender ran his eye over Chet.

'Sure, Frank,' she replied. 'This is Chet Hallam, an old friend of mine from my Texas days. His father is Arch Hallam, our sheriff until he disappeared last month.'

Frank nodded, his expression changing, and he cut short something he was saying and went back to the bar. Chet watched him speculatively. He switched his gaze to Maisie and saw she was watching him closely, her blue eyes showing traces of fear.

'You're in the thick of things around here,' he said. 'Just like the old days in Texas, huh? What can you tell me about the local set-up?'

'Chet, when I left Texas I gave up on that way of life. What happened there made a big impression on me, and I've been on the straight and narrow ever since.'

He smiled and nodded. 'I'll believe you, Maisie, but thousands wouldn't. Seriously, I'm gonna find out what happened to my pa, so if you are caught up in anything around here then now is the time to get out. Is that clear?'

'I swear to God, Chet. I'm straight now. I'm a singer, and that's as far as it goes. Give me a break and don't tell anyone that you caught me fair and square back in Texas. That happened a long time ago, and I learned my lesson the hard way.'

'I said I believe you, Maisie. Drop it now. But I'd appreciate it, if you do decide to get out, if you'd give me the low-down on the local situation before you leave.'

'I have to sing another song now,' she said hurriedly, getting to her feet. 'I guess you'll want to see me later, huh?'

'I surely will,' he replied.

'I was afraid of that!' She put on her smile and left him gazing after her.

Sol Kennedy was waiting for Maisie by the piano

and, by the expression on his face, the lawman was not pleased that Maisie had sat down with Chet. He wagged a finger under her nose and, when she turned away from him to speak to the pianist, Kennedy came towards Chet's table, his face wearing a thundercloud expression and his right hand resting on the butt of his holstered gun.

Chet dropped his right hand below the level of the table and touched the butt of his holstered pistol. He had a feeling that he would need it. Kennedy looked like a man who had a bad case of jealousy. . . .

TWO

Kennedy paused beside Chet's table. He was breathing heavily. Chet continued eating his meal, and the deputy dropped into the seat Maisie had occupied and leaned his elbows on the table. He gazed into Chet's face for several moments, his mouth twisted by the unpleasant emotions pulsing through his mind. Chet ignored him; chewed his beef steak with relish.

'Maisie said you two knew each other in Texas,' said Kennedy in a cold, sneering tone. 'Was she your gal?'

Chet gazed at the deputy for several moments while he finished his mouthful of steak. When he had swallowed the beef he put down his fork.

'You're certainly a man who loves asking questions,' he observed. 'But give me a break. This is the first food I've eaten since sun-up, and I'd like to enjoy it peaceful like. If you want to talk to me then wait until I've finished here.'

'You're walking a thin line,' Kennedy grated.

'You're getting into my hair, mister, and I don't like it. Maisie is my gal, see? And I ain't happy about drifters who knew her back in Texas showing up again and trying to horn in.'

'Where'd you get the idea from that I might be interested in Maisie?' Chet picked up his fork and waved it in Kennedy's face. 'My taste in women doesn't include Maisie.'

'Are you saying that Maisie ain't all right because she sings in a saloon?'

'You said that! Are you trying to pick a fight with me?' Chet countered.

Kennedy cursed and stood up abruptly. Chet's right hand disappeared under the table. He expected gun play. But Kennedy grasped the edge of the table and up-ended it with a furious jerk, hurling it forward against Chet, sending the dinner plate on it up against Chet's chest. Chet went over backwards, overturning his chair. He rolled clear and got to his feet, his gaze on Kennedy. The deputy set his right hand in motion and reached for his holstered gun, triggering Chet into furious action. Chet's gun hand went to his pistol with practised ease and speed.

Mindful that Kennedy was a lawman, Chet drew his gun so fast it was cocked and levelled at Kennedy's chest before the deputy could clear leather. Kennedy halted his draw, his face blanching. His expression changed from fury to fear, and his mouth gaped as he realized that he was well and truly beaten.

'You just made a bad mistake, Kennedy,' Chet said

harshly. 'If you're still of a mind to play with your gun then we can start again, but the next time I'll squeeze my trigger. I'll overlook what you did to my meal, and if you've got any sense you'll ease your gun out of leather, drop it on the floor, and then get the hell out of here.'

There was silence in the saloon. Maisie had started singing but she fell silent when the table was up-ended. Kennedy's face turned from ashen to dull red. He was in two minds about his next action. He had the impulse to continue his draw, but common sense overcame his emotion and he lifted his pistol out of its holster, using index finger and thumb only, and then dropped it to the floor. He turned silently, walked to the batwings, and departed.

Chet waited with his gun covering the batwings. When he heard Kennedy's boots receding on the boardwalk he put away his pistol. The waitress appeared at his side as he righted the table and picked up the chair. Her face was pale.

'I'm sorry about your meal,' she said. 'Shall I bring you another steak?'

'No, don't bother,' he replied. 'I was almost finished, anyway. But I'll have a helping of apple pie and a cup of coffee.'

He sat down at the table as if nothing had happened, and the saloon came back to life. He noticed that Maisie didn't finish her song, and now she was nowhere in sight. He sat motionless, taking an occasional mouthful of the fresh beer, which the 'tender quickly brought over. He watched the man clean up the wreckage of the meal. The waitress returned with the balance of his meal, and Chet ate it. When he had finished, he paid and tipped the waitress, got to his feet, and departed. He cleared the batwings, stepped quickly to one side and dropped to one knee. A split second later, the bullet that came out of the shadows missed him by a scant inch and embedded itself in the woodwork behind him. He threw himself flat, and his gun was back in his hand as he looked around for the source of the shot. Muzzle flame had spurted from an alley mouth across the street, and gun smoke drifted in front of a lantern hanging in a dark corner.

Chet moved quickly. He rolled off the sidewalk into the thick dust of the street. The gun across the way cut loose again, and several slugs hammered into the ground around Chet's fast-moving figure. He came up into the aim and triggered three spaced shots that bracketed the opposite shadows. He moved again before he prepared for another shot. He heard running feet, and looked up to see a figure, holding a gun, coming towards him from across the street. He flipped up his pistol into the aim and fired two quick shots.

The running man jerked and hesitated as hot lead struck him. The pistol he was holding clattered to the street. He twisted but maintained his forward motion. Lantern light glinted on the gun in the dust. Chet held his fire, watching. The man came on for two more strides, and then his legs gave way and he sprawled headlong into the dust. He did not move again.

27

Chet got slowly to his feet, gun ready for action. But the hostility was over. Gun echoes faded away across the town. Men began to ease out of the saloon, crowding on the sidewalk. Chet saw a figure approaching him on the boards to his left and swung his gun to cover it.

'Hold your fire, Hallam,' the man called. 'This is Sol Kennedy. What in hell is going on?'

'Someone took shots at me from cover when I came out of the saloon,' Chet replied. 'I figured it was you, Kennedy.'

'Not guilty!' The deputy came to Chet's side. He was holding a small hideout gun, and thrust the muzzle towards Chet. 'Smell it,' he said harshly. 'My back-up gun; it hasn't been fired in a week.'

Chet took the weapon and lifted the muzzle to his nose. It was clean – smelled of oil not gun smoke. He returned it to Kennedy, who kept it in his hand and went towards the unmoving figure sprawled in the street. Chet followed, watching his surroundings. Kennedy bent over the still figure, and then dragged it around slightly so that the light of a nearby lantern illuminated its face.

'Jeez!' he ejaculated. 'It's Waco Sim!'

'Who was he when he was alive?' Chet demanded.

'Nobody much!' Kennedy uttered a short, harsh laugh. 'Sim spent most of his time in the saloon, and the rest of it doing odd jobs to buy whiskey. He didn't work much, so he stole where he could and rubbed along from day to day. Folks never offered him work because he was unreliable.'

28

'So he was trying to earn money by shooting me?' Chet demanded.

'Who knows you're around? You only got here today,' Kennedy responded.

Chet did not answer. He holstered his gun and turned away, heading along the sidewalk to the end of the street where the shacks were. He stepped into a doorway and reloaded the empty chambers in his pistol, and then continued, and was relieved to reach his mother's shack without further incident.

Mrs Hallam was tense and highly nervous when she opened the door to him. She was a tall, slim lady, her appeal overburdened by her worry over her missing husband. Chet smiled reassuringly at her, entered the shack, and watched her bar the stout door.

'I heard shooting a while back,' she said. 'Were you involved, Chet?'

'No, Ma, not this time! The deputy had to subdue a drunk. The town is quiet again now. I'm trying to piece together what's been going on around here. Let's sit down and talk. I'm groping in the dark. Tell me about Pa. Why did he pull out like he did? And why doesn't anyone know where he has gone?'

'He never told me anything about his job,' she replied, shaking her head. 'And most of the time I was afraid to ask him. All I knew was that it was a highly dangerous way of life. There was always trouble in the county, and he never had enough help to handle it the way it should have been. He spent a lot of time at night out around the town, looking for

29

trouble, and he arrested some hard cases. But he couldn't get to grips with the big trouble.'

'And that's the best you can tell me, huh?' he demanded when she fell silent. 'Ma, I'm your son. When I came into town, the first thing I heard was that Pa disappeared a month ago. The few folks I've talked to can't or won't tell me anything, and now you're giving me wrong impressions about Pa's life. What are you afraid of? Who has put the freeze on you? Don't you care what's happened to Pa? Or do you know for certain he's dead? I can tell you're holding out on me about something.'

'Your pa must have had a good reason for pulling out like he did.' She shook her head. 'I don't believe he's dead. He had a lot on his mind, and felt he had to get away for a spell. I have to believe that or I'll go loco.'

'I can't believe he'd go without telling you why, Ma. You're his wife, for God's sake! Level with me and I'll get to work and make it right for Pa to come back.'

'Face up to it, Chet. Deep down, I fear Pa is dead.'

Chet gazed at his mother, unable to believe what she was saying. His thoughts were quick and deep, like a mountain torrent after a flash flood. He shook his head slowly, his face harsh, his eyes bleak.

'I'll never believe Pa ran out like you said,' he observed. 'He wasn't a man like that. He'd die before leaving you high and dry. Where is Arnie? He always caused trouble in the family, if I remember rightly. I'll bet he's mixed up in this somewhere. Pa was

30

always getting him out of a tight spot, and Arnie never liked Pa. He hated you remarrying after his own father was killed, and hated my pa for taking his place.'

'Arnie's in town, living in a guest house. He's going to marry Annie, the daughter of Matt Lomax, who owns the stage line and the stable here in town. He stayed away from your father, so I never saw much of him after we got here, but I'm glad he's doing all right.'

'Where will I find him? I'll need to talk to him.'

'It would be better to stay well away from him. Don't tangle with him, Chet.'

'He's my brother, and I'll likely need his help to get a lead on what's going on around here.'

'He's staying at the Gibson guest house. It's next to Polly's dress shop. I wish you wouldn't see him, Chet!'

'To tell the truth I'm not too happy to meet up with him again, but it looks like I've got no choice.'

'He may be away on a riding job.'

'I can find out about that from his boss. And I need to find a place where I can hit the sack. You don't have any room for me to stay here.'

'I had to leave our house after Pa went so the new sheriff could move in. This is the best I could find at short notice.'

'I'll see about getting a house tomorrow, and we can move in together. What do you say to that?'

'It sounds lovely, Chet.'

'I'll look in on you tomorrow, Ma.' Chet got to his

feet and moved to the door.

'Take care,' she warned. 'If something bad has happened to Pa then the men who did it won't want you nosing around.'

'Don't worry about me, Ma.' He laughed: a harsh sound. 'I can take care of myself, and then some.'

He was disappointed as he went back into town, but he could understand his mother's attitude. She was alone. His father was no longer around to protect her.

He found the stage line's office next to the bank, and there was a light burning in the front room. He knocked at the door, and several moments passed before a cautious voice demanded to know who was there.

'I'm Chet Hallam, Arnie's brother,' he replied. 'I need to talk to Arnie urgently.'

There was the sound of a key being turned in a lock and the scrape of bolts withdrawing. The door swung open and Chet gazed into an older man's haggard face that wore an expression of deep despair. Dark eyes gazed at him suspiciously. A wispy, greying beard covered the chin. The man was tall, about six feet, and he was thin, as if he had been missing most of his meals. He was dressed in a good town suit of light blue material.

'Are you really Arnie's brother?' he demanded.

'Yeah, I'm Chet Hallam. I got in from Texas a short while ago.'

'I've heard Arnie talking about a brother down in Texas. What's brought you up this way, son?'

'You must have heard that my father has gone missing. I've come to find him.'

The door opened wider. 'I'm Matt Lomax. You better come inside. I told Arnie yesterday to stay out of Spruce Bend for a time. Since your father went missing my two coaches have been held up and robbed, and Arnie has been threatened. If he doesn't get out until the heat is over he'll be killed. He's a fighter, but he's outnumbered, and if he doesn't lie low now they'll surely kill him.'

'Why are feelings running high about my father? Wasn't he a good lawman?'

'He was, and that's the trouble. The bad men are trying to take over in this county. Mitch Frazee runs a bad bunch around here, and nobody can stop him. Sheriff Hallam had several fights with the gang, but he was only one man, and he didn't get much help from folks who should have backed him. It's a real sorry business.'

'So where is Arnie now?'

'He brought a stage in yesterday, nursing a bullet wound in his right arm. The strong box was taken in a hold-up, and Bill Wiskin, the shotgun guard, was killed. I can't continue to run the business much longer. I'm thinking of cutting my losses, and I reckon I'll be lucky if I can get out with my life.'

'And Arnie?' Chet demanded.

Lomax shook his head. 'He ain't left town. That's the word I've put around to keep the heat off him. He's in hiding until his arm heals. He can't use a gun right now. I'm putting him up in my home. He and my daughter Annie are planning to get married in September. Look, I'm just about through here for the day. Come home with me and you'll be able to see Arnie.'

Chet nodded, and took a seat while Lomax put away the ledgers he had been working on and tidied up the office.

'We'll leave by the back door,' Lomax said, picking up a shotgun from a corner and checking its loads. 'I've got a feeling I'm a marked man now, so I have to take precautions. Say, Arnie told me you were a Texas Ranger, so you must have left your job to come north. Will you consider coming to work for me? I'll pay top wages.'

'At the moment my mind won't stretch past the fact that my father is missing – might be dead. I'm going all out to find out what happened to him.'

'Well, bear in mind that I need a good man. I might be able to carry on my business if I can fight off Frazee's gang.'

They left the office by the back door, and Chet was instantly plunged into darkness. He halted, trying to pierce the night. The shadows were so dense he could have carved his name on them. Lomax spoke from only feet away, and Chat could barely see his outline.

'I'm afraid to carry a lantern,' said Lomax, his voice sounding disembodied in the night. 'I doubt I'd get to the house without being shot at.'

'What's the law doing about your problems?' Chet demanded.

'The short answer is – nothing! Oh, the sheriff has been out time and again with a posse, but they don't have any luck. It's like that all over the county. Buck Allen took over as sheriff after your father disappeared, and he does his best, which ain't good enough.'

'And my father didn't do any better when he was in office, huh?'

'He did what he could, but no one can beat the situation we've got here. Come this way. It's pretty good underfoot. The house is fifty yards back from here, and there's a regular pathway.'

Chet's eyes slowly became accustomed to the darkness, and he was able to see Lomax's tall figure in front of him. They crossed the back lot, and Chet was unable to see the lights of the Lomax house. He was beginning to think there was no house when they arrived at a building; from close up Chet could see chinks of light piercing the wooden shutters that had been closed over all the lower windows.

Lomax unlocked the front door and they entered a long hall, which was illuminated by a lamp. A girl appeared from a room towards the rear of the house and came towards them.

'Annie, call Arnie. This is his brother Chet. He's just got in from Texas.'

'You don't look much like Arnie,' Annie countered.

'We're stepbrothers.' Chet admired Arnie's choice for a wife. Annie was tall and slim in a pale blue satin dress that revealed the curves of a good figure. She

35

had brown hair, was very good-looking, and her eyes were a light shade of blue. She held out her hand and Chet shook it. 'I'm pleased to meet you, Annie,' he continued.

'I don't know if Arnie will be pleased to see you, Chet,' she replied. 'I've heard him talking about you many times, and I've got the feeling there's bad blood between the two of you.'

'Not from my side,' Chet said quickly. 'Arnie's had a chip on his shoulder for as long as I can remember. His father died when Arnie was three years old, and our mother married my father a year later. I always regarded Arnie as a brother. But he didn't have similar feelings. I didn't know he was a stepbrother until I was about fifteen. The ill-feeling he suffers is all on his side.'

'We all have our faults,' Lomax opined. 'I've always found him reliable, and he's a good worker. He's brought the coach through several ambushes, and only once lost a strong box. He picked up a nasty wound yesterday.'

'He's resting in bed at the moment.' Annie turned to ascend the stairs. 'I'll see if he's awake.'

'Don't disturb him now,' Chet said quickly. 'I'll catch up with him tomorrow.'

'You've found your mother?' Annie asked.

'Yes. I'm gonna rent a house in town. Ma shouldn't be in that shack.'

'We suggested that she come here to live when your father disappeared but she wouldn't even consider it,' Lomax said.

Chet smiled. 'She's too independent for her own good.' He turned to the door. 'It's been nice meeting you,' he declared. 'I'll be on my way now. Tell Arnie I'll be around to see him in the morning.'

Lomax reached out to open the front door, and froze when a heavy hand knocked on the woodwork outside. He stepped back a pace and lifted his shotgun. He glanced at Chet, his eyes filled with apprehension.

'Who's out there?' he called, thumbing back the hammers on the shotgun.

'Sheriff Allen,' a harsh voice replied. 'Open the door, Matt. I need to talk to you.'

Relief sprang into Lomax's eyes as he eased forward the hammers on his gun. Chet could see that he was under great strain. Lomax lowered the shotgun and tucked the butt into his right armpit. He reached out with his left hand, opened the door, and a big man wearing a law star on his shirt front stepped forward into the lamplight issuing through the doorway.

'It's a helluva business when a man has to answer his door with a loaded shotgun in his hands,' the sheriff declared. He looked into Chet's eyes. 'I'm Buck Allen.' He held out his right hand. 'You're Chet Hallam, I guess. Sorry I missed you when you came to the office. I'd like you to come and see me in the morning.'

'Sure.' Chet shook the proffered hand.

The sheriff was a tall, powerful man aged around forty years. His face had some spare flesh around the jaw line, and his blue eyes glittered like shards of broken glass in the lamplight. He was wearing brown pants and a green shirt; the legs of his pants were tucked into brown riding boots. He looked competent, and had an edge to his easy manner. Chet noticed that his smile did not reach his eyes, and his friendly tone sounded false. Although he was smiling, he had the look of a lobo wolf about him. Chet kept his face expressionless, but alarm bells were ringing in his mind.

'Any time after sun up will find me in the law office,' Allen said. He turned his attention to Lomax. 'I need to have a few more words with Arnie to clear up a couple of points.'

'I'll fetch him down,' Annie said instantly, and began to ascend the stairs, but she halted on the bottom stair when a hard-toned voice spoke above her head.

'Hold your horses, Annie. I'm coming down. It's no use trying to rest with all the noise going on down there. It sounds like a meeting of the Women's League.'

Chet watched the stairs. The lamplight reached no higher than halfway up. He saw a pair of legs appear and descend slowly until Arnie came fully into view. Chet realized that he was holding his breath, and released it silently. He had not seen Arnie in five years, and his stepbrother now looked a lot older. He was heavier by several pounds, and looked careworn. His black hair had become sparse and straggly. He was tall and well-built, but still as handsome as ever, although he seemed flabby. His right shoulder was heavily bandaged, and he was holding his left hand under his right elbow to give support to his injured limb.

Arnie paused on the bottom stair and gazed at Chet for a lingering moment, and then smiled humourlessly.

'I've been expecting you to show up around here,' he said sharply.

'That wouldn't have taken much to work out,' Chet answered. 'It was my father that disappeared. My guess is you didn't have much to do with him from the time the family settled down here.'

'Arch never had much time for me!'

'That could have been because you never accepted him as a father. . . .'

'I heard at an early age that he was the lawman who killed my father!'

'You're still the same old Arnie.' Chet shook his head. 'I'm sick of making excuses for your behaviour. Listen, all I want to know from you is if you have any idea what happened to Arch.'

'I don't know, and what's more, I don't care. Our trails never crossed around here. I heard he had vanished, but he was nothing to me. Sorry I can't help you.' Arnie smiled coldly and looked at the watching sheriff. 'What do you want now?' he demanded. 'Not more useless questions! You couldn't catch those outlaws if they fell out of the sky on top of you.'

'I'm only doing my duty as I see it,' Allen said roughly. 'I'm being run ragged by Frazee and his bunch. I need all the help I can get if I'm ever gonna beat him, and you have had several run-ins with him.'

'He nearly killed me yesterday.' Tension sounded in Arnie's tone. 'I've told you all I know, so why don't you leave me alone?'

'We'll all feel a lot better when that thieving gang of killers is put where it belongs.' Allen sounded as if he had reached the end of his patience. 'You better start doing like I tell you if you don't want me to haul you into the jail and tie you down until you do give me all the facts about the hold-up. So you're a big hero now, making a stand against the hard bunch, but the rest of us have to plod on trying to make something out of nothing if we're ever gonna nail the gang.'

'Just give me a break, will you?' Arnie demanded. 'I'll drop by your office tomorrow. Will that do?'

'Yeah, so long as you keep your word. I don't wanta have to come for you again.'

'I'll be along around ten.' Arnie continued back up the stairs and Annie followed him, glancing apologetically at Chet, who remained motionless until a door upstairs slammed.

Sheriff Allen was already leaving. He paused with the door open and glanced at Chet.

'Call in and see me as early as you can make it tomorrow,' he said.

Chet nodded and the lawman departed. Lomax closed the door quickly and locked it, gripping his shotgun tightly.

'It looks like you're gonna be as popular around

here as Arnie,' he observed. 'Don't forget that I've got a good job for you, and I think my offer will be better than any other that might come your way.'

Chet nodded and departed. He felt uneasy about the way Arnie was reacting to the situation, and he guessed that whatever job he took he would find himself knee-deep in trouble and life would be anything but dull. . . .

THREE

Chet went back to Main Street and entered the hotel. The effects of his trail from Texas lay heavily on his shoulders. His head was teeming with thoughts, and he was unhappy about the situation that had enveloped him. He saw a tall young woman at the reception desk, who smiled a welcome when she looked up and saw him. Her teeth were small, even, and exceptionally white. The smile reached her blue eyes, put glints in their pale depths, and Chet responded instinctively.

'I've stayed in a lot of hotels in my time!' he exclaimed. 'But I've never seen a more welcoming smile than yours, Miss. You must attract business like a honey pot in high summer.'

'Good evening, I'm Ellen Whiteside,' she greeted in a pleasant voice, her smile widening. 'My father owns the hotel. How may I help you?'

'I'm Chet Hallam,' he replied. 'I need a room at least for one night.'

'Are you just passing through, Mr Hallam?'

He shook his head. 'My father was the sheriff here until he disappeared about a month ago. I've come up from Texas to find out what happened to him.'

'That is a bad business,' she assured him quickly, 'and it must be worrying your mother.'

He nodded, his smile diminishing.

'Please sign the register.' She turned to a key board. 'I'll put you in Number Ten. It gives a fine view of Main Street.'

He signed the register and she held out a key.

'I hope you will enjoy your stay in town,' she said. 'Your room is up the stairs – the second door on the left.'

'I'll pick up the key later. I've got to collect my saddlebags. Thank you.'

He left, her smile an image in his mind. He walked along the sidewalk to the shacks to collect his saddlebags and, when he saw the door of his mother's shack was open, he ran forward, his mind fully alert. A shadow moved towards him from the darkness beside the open door, and he caught the glint of lamplight on a gun in a man's hand, the weapon uplifted to strike him a blow.

Chet did not break his stride. He stepped inside the arc that brought the weapon swiftly to his head, blocked the blow, and delivered a powerful short right-hand punch to the man's jaw. He drew his gun as the man went down, and stepped into the open doorway of the shack. His mother was cowering in a seat at the table, and a man was standing over her, one hand raised menacingly, his face turned towards the door.

43

When the man saw Chet he reached for his gun. Chet cocked his weapon and levelled it.

'Pull it and I'll kill you,' Chet said.

The man froze, pistol half-drawn. He hesitated before thrusting the weapon deep into its holster.

'Who are you and what are you doing in here?' Chet said, and continued, before the man could answer, 'Get rid of your gun and then step outside and pick up your sidekick. Bring him in here.'

The man, a tall, heavy individual, dressed in range clothes, lifted his gun from its holster and laid it on the table at his side. He stepped outside, and Chet followed him. The second man, unconscious on the ground, was lifted and dragged into the shack. Chet closed the door. He moved to the chair in which his mother was seated.

'Are you OK, Ma?' he asked, his attention on the intruders.

She nodded, too shocked to speak. Chet turned his attention to the men.

'What's going on?' he asked. 'How come you're in here, threatening my mother?'

'We brought a message for the lady,' said the hard case Chet had disarmed.

'When I came into the doorway it looked as if you were menacing her. What's your name, mister, and what's your business?'

'I don't have to answer your questions,' the man replied.

'Don't try my patience,' Chet warned. 'Get your pard on his feet and we'll head for the jail.'

'I told you, we only came to deliver a message. There ain't no need to drag the law into this.'

'What was he saying to you when I came in, Ma?' Chet asked.

'I really couldn't say,' she replied in a trembling tone. 'I was so scared, my brain went numb. I thought I heard Arnie's name mentioned, but I can't be sure.'

'OK. Lock the door when we leave, and don't open it again to anyone but me. I'll sing out when I get back.'

The unconscious man was beginning to regain his senses. Chet ushered them out of the shack, and paused until he heard the door being locked and bolted.

'Get moving,' he said. 'You must know where the jail is so let's go talk to the sheriff. If you've got any ideas about getting the better of me then forget them, because I'm hoping you'll try something so I can kill you.'

They headed for the jail. Sol Kennedy was standing in the shadows at the main entrance, smoking a cigar, and he stepped forward when he saw two men approaching him with their hands up above their shoulders.

'What's going on here?' Kennedy demanded, drawing his pistol.

'I came across these two menacing my mother in her shack,' Chet said. 'They didn't want to talk to me so I brought them along here. Do you know them?'

'I wish I didn't! The one on the right is Billy

45

Redfern and the other is Shep Barrett. They're a couple of the bunch who hang out with Joe Hoyt, the banker's son. They don't have to work for their living, so they've got plenty of time to get into trouble. You broke Hoyt's jaw, as I recall, so I suspect they were calling on you. Need I say more?'

'You've said enough,' Chet replied. 'They were looking for me.'

'Let's get them up in the law office and I'll talk to them,' Kennedy said. 'I've been trying to pin something on this pair for a long time. Barrett's father owns the Circle B cow spread north of town.'

They went up to the law office and the jailer admitted them. Kennedy searched Redfern and Barrett, removing their possessions from their pockets.

'There's no need for this,' Barrett complained. 'We were only delivering a message to Mrs Hallam. We needed to know where her son Arnie was hiding himself.'

'What would you want with him?' Kennedy's voice was harsh. 'You two have been running wild around the county for some time now, and you're gonna pull in your horns after this.' He glanced at Chet. 'Is your mother gonna make a charge against them?'

Chet shrugged. 'It's too early to say. They scared the hell out of her, and Barrett was standing over her when I entered the shack, his hand raised in a threatening manner. If Ma doesn't make a charge then I'll see the pair of them through gun smoke.'

'So I'll put them in a cell until sun up,' Kennedy decided. 'Come and see me in the morning and let

46

me know if there will be charges.' He glanced at the attentive jailer. 'Put 'em in a cage, Pete. Maybe they'll be more helpful tomorrow.'

Chet remained until the two men were taken into the cell block before departing. He went back to the shack, and Mrs Hallam admitted him. She was still pale and shocked, and did not answer Chet's questions about the incident. He changed the subject when he noted her manner.

'I saw Arnie a short while ago,' he told her. 'He hasn't mellowed over the past five years. Still the same old Arnie! I'll stay away from him in future.' He sat down at the table. 'I'd like you to come to the hotel with me, Ma, just for tonight. I'm worried about you, and I'll sleep easier if you're not here alone.'

'I'll be all right, Chet. Don't worry about me.' She looked at him, and worry showed in her eyes. 'I wish Pa was here. He would know what to do. Why did he run away? He was never a man like that. He faced up to problems when he was younger.'

'Is there anything you're not telling me about the situation? I've got the feeling you're holding something back, Ma, and at the moment I need all the help I can get. Give me a break. I must have the truth about everything.'

'I know nothing that could help you,' she replied, shaking her head.

'All right, we'll leave it there for now. But I insist you come to the hotel with me, so put a few things in a bag and let's go. Tomorrow we'll see about getting us a house, and then I'll be able to keep an eye on you.'

She shook her head, but Chet would not take a negative answer from her, and she finally broke her resistance and got up to prepare for a night in the hotel. He sighed with relief when she locked the door of the shack and accompanied him along the street. They entered the hotel, and Ellen Whiteside soon eased Mrs Hallam's mind and installed her in the room next to Chet's. He waited until his mother felt easy enough to be left and went into his own room.

He settled down for the night, his mind overstretched with worry, filled with wondering about what had happened to his father. Knowing his father as he did, he feared the worst. Arch Hallam would never run away from anything, and he could only assume that the old man was dead, but he would not rest until he had discovered the truth behind his father's disappearance.

He lay staring up into the darkness, trying to work out the best way to tackle the problem, and fell asleep still struggling mentally. When he awoke, the grey light of dawn was pressing against the window, and he arose to start the new day, eager to get to grips with the mystery of his father's disappearance, yet half afraid of what he might uncover.

He left his room and paused outside the door of his mother's room – listened intently for sounds coming from inside, but heard nothing. He wanted to see Sheriff Allen, and went down to the dining room to find Ellen Whiteside setting the tables for breakfast.

'You start early in the day, Miss Whiteside,' he observed.

'That's the nature of the business, Mr Hallam,' she replied, smiling. 'Is Mrs Hallam still asleep?'

'I didn't hear any noise coming from her room, although I remember she was always an early riser.'

'She had quite a fright last evening. Is she going back to her shack this morning?'

'I hope not, but I'm afraid she will. I'd like her to stay on here for a few days until I can find a house to rent.'

'Perhaps I can help you there. We own several houses in the quieter part of town, and I do know one became vacant a couple of weeks ago. If you'd like to look at it, and find it suitable, I'll be pleased to rent it to you.'

'Thank you. I'll take you up on your offer. I'm going along to the law office now. I have to see the sheriff. If my mother comes asking for me, tell her I'll be back shortly, and perhaps we'll look at the house as soon as possible.'

'I'll watch for your mother, and keep an eye on her until you get back.'

Chet thanked her and departed. He went to the law office. The jailer opened the door to him.

'You won't be pleased by my news,' said Peter Sayer, rattling the bunch of keys. 'We lost Shep Barrett in the night. He tore a couple of boards out of the ceiling of his cell, removed some shingles, got

49

out on the roof, and then lost his balance. He landed on his head in the street, and we didn't need Doc Fletcher to tell us he was dead. Redfern didn't go with him. He's still in the cells. Kennedy has ridden out to the Circle B to tell Barrett's father what happened.'

Chet was shocked by the news. He went to the cell, now empty, and saw how Barrett had escaped. Sayer took him to another cell, where Billy Redfern was sleeping restlessly on a bunk. Chet went back to the office. Sayer accompanied him, still jangling his keys.

'Is the sheriff around?' Chet asked. 'He wants to see me this morning. He said to be early.'

'I ain't set eyes on him yet.' Sayer shook his head. 'He told me you'd be showing up. You'll have to wait for him to show.'

'I want to start investigating my father's disappearance. What can you tell me about Waco Sim?'

'I heard he tried to kill you last night.' Sayer nodded. 'I guess he must have had a good reason for shooting at you, so you'd do well to check on his recent activities. He's been on the fringe of lawlessness ever since he showed up in town a couple of years ago. He was a man who never worked regularly but always had money in his pocket. I'd guess if anyone around here had anything to do with your father's disappearance then Waco would be a good place to start asking questions.'

'Was he ever caught breaking the law?'

'He was jailed several times for being drunk and disorderly, but nothing of a criminal nature. He was

50

too sharp to get caught – if he was ever involved in anything crooked.'

'Did he have any friends in town?'

'None I knew of. He was shacked up with Jane Terrill, whose husband was hanged two years ago for killing a man and stealing his horse. I don't know how she'll get on now Waco's dead. Come to think of it, Waco always had enough money to pay their way around town. It might be as well to check up on where he was getting his dough from. Jane lives in one of those shacks where your mother is – about four doors further along.'

'That's where I intend starting. Waco shot at me because someone paid him to do it or he had other reasons of his own. I need to find out what was in his mind.'

'You're pretty smart, I guess.' Sayer grinned. 'They told me you'd been a Texas Ranger for five years, and lawmen don't come any smarter or tougher than those guys. Good luck to you. I liked your father. He was a straight shooter, and honest as the day is long. He stepped on a few toes while he was the sheriff, and maybe that was why he disappeared.'

'So what is going on around here?'

'How do you mean?'

'On the face of it, there's no crime beyond rustling, although there's an outlaw gang in the county, bossed by Mitch Frazee. So what caused my father's disappearance? What's hidden in the wood-pile, huh?'

'I never looked at it like that.' Sayer rubbed his

chin. 'I do know that if you turn over any stone you'll always find something crawling underneath it.'

'Hey, Pete, open up.' Buck Allen's voice had the jailer jumping up from his seat and hurrying to the barred entrance.

Chet remained thoughtful, mentally chafing at the situation. The sheriff came into the office and sat down at the desk. He looked as if he hadn't slept during the night. His eyes were red-rimmed. He stifled a yawn as he gazed at Chet.

'Things have sure started happening since you showed up in town,' he observed.

'Not my trouble,' Chet countered. 'It's more like something's been waiting for my arrival. So what was my father involved in a month ago? Spruce Bend looks like any other town in the county – quiet, filled with good folk going about their lawful lives, but there's an undercurrent of lawlessness here which has enveloped some of the men and forced them to overstep the bounds of their lives. My father, for instance, a lawful man by nature, has disappeared, apparently for no good reason. Waco Sim shot at me, although we were strangers. Then Redfern and Barratt showed up at my mother's shack. I brought them in here for questioning, and Barrett died trying to escape.'

'Yeah, I guess there is more going on around here than meets the eye. That's why I want you as a deputy. I'm looking ahead right now, and I don't like what I see. You're an experienced lawman, and you've got a personal interest in what's going on. So will you pin on a deputy star? You can root around the mystery of your father's disappearance with a free hand, and I'll be mighty surprised if you don't get your teeth into something that will open a whole can of beans.'

'I'll need to think about it,' Chet said. 'I don't want to be tied down by the job, although a law badge would give me some weight in the county.'

'Pin on a badge,' Allen urged. 'You can always hand it in if you find it restricts you. What have you got to lose? It will give you the right to ask questions of anyone in the community, but if you go nosing around without authority you'd soon run into trouble with the law, which would bring you up against me.'

'OK.' Chet shrugged. 'I guess I've got nothing to lose. Swear me in and let me get to work.'

'Raise your right hand.' Allen opened a drawer, produced a deputy law star, and gabbled through the oath.

Chet agreed to obey, and pinned the star to his shirt front.

'That's mighty fine.' Allen grinned, looking relieved at having recruited Chet to the local law department. 'That's all there is to it,' he continued. 'Now you can go out and show your teeth to all those lawbreakers around town. I'll back you all the way. Just don't shoot the mayor or any other prominent citizen. You know how the law works – it's the same whether you're here or in Texas. Have you any questions?'

'Not right now. I'll play it by ear, which means

asking questions of my own. I'll check with you if I learn anything.'

'I wish you luck, but I've been over every aspect of your father's case, and I don't mind telling you that I'm baffled. I'm just hoping you'll come up with something.'

Chet nodded and left the office. He heaved a sigh of relief when he was standing on the sidewalk looking around the street. But duty could wait a little longer, he thought. He'd had no breakfast, and needed to check on his mother. He crossed the street to the hotel.

Mrs Hallam was seated in the dining room with Ellen Whiteside. Both were eating breakfast. Chet joined them, and Ellen fetched him some food. His mother saw the law star on his shirt and shook her head.

'You're not going to disappear like your father did, are you?' she demanded.

'Not if I can help it,' he replied. 'This is the only way I'll be able to make any headway. I've got one or two leads to follow up, but I think too much time has passed since Pa's disappearance. The trail has gone cold.'

'He was in a hurry to get on the trail that day he disappeared, and got up from the table immediately after finishing his breakfast. I haven't seen him since.' Mrs Hallam's tone changed as she switched subjects abruptly. 'Ellen has asked me to stay here for a couple of days. She needs a hand around the place, and I don't have enough to occupy my mind at the shack.'

'That's a good idea.' Chet nodded. 'I'll look in and check on you from time to time.'

He took his leave and went along the sidewalk to the shacks on the outskirts of the town. He selected the shack he wanted and knocked on the door. There was no reply. He knocked again, more forcefully, and moments later the door was opened by a tall, thin blonde woman whose face was harshly set in grief. Her eyes were red-rimmed, filled with pain. She was in a pink housecoat and had no shoes on her feet. She stared at him in silence, and he waited for her to speak. When she continued to remain silent he cleared his throat.

'You're Jane Terrill?' he asked. 'I'm Chet Hallam. I've just been taken on as a deputy. I understand that Waco Sim lived here, and I'd like to ask you some questions about him.'

She began to weep, and produced a wisp of handkerchief to wipe her eyes. Chet waited, and when she replaced the handkerchief in her pocket, he continued: 'Waco didn't have a regular job, I understand. Can I come in and talk to you about him?'

She opened the door wide and stepped backwards a couple of paces. Chet entered the shack and she closed the door. He looked around. The interior was a mess. It had not been cleaned in days, the blankets on the bed in a corner were rumpled; dirty plates and dishes were lying on the table. The window was tightly closed, and the place smelled as if it had not been aired in a month.

'I'm sorry to have to call on you at a time like this,'

Chet said gently, 'but Waco tried to shoot a man last night, a stranger, and for no apparent reason. Have you any idea why he would do that? What was he involved in around here?'

Jane sat down on a chair at the table and hunched her shoulders. She sniffed loudly, but said nothing. She produced the handkerchief again, and began to cry softly.

'I don't know anything about what Waco did,' she said in a quavering voice. 'He never told me anything, and if I asked questions he hit me.'

'He must have talked about some of the things he was doing,' Chet prompted. 'Was he a criminal? Where did he get his money from?'

She shook her head and did not reply. Chet studied her for several moments, aware that he would learn nothing while she was in her present state.

'Did he have any friends in town?'

'Not that I know of,' she replied.

'Perhaps I'd better come back later, when you've had time to recover from the shock you've had. I'll probably be able to get the information I want from other folks. Waco was well known in town.'

'And what you'll hear from other folks will be a pack of lies,' she retorted. 'No one liked Waco, and they all gave him a bad name. But he wasn't like that. He was a good man.'

'He tried to murder a stranger – which is not the action of a good man. Why don't you tell me about him?'

56

She shook her head. 'I can't talk about him now. I'm too badly shocked. The doctor gave me some medicine to take, and I hardly know what I'm saying.'

Chet shook his head and took his leave. He walked the length of Main Street and entered the livery barn. Five range-clad men were putting their horses into stalls. One of them, older than the other four and more expensively dressed, looked up at Chet, noted his law star, and came to confront him, his face set in grim lines. His pale blue eyes were glinting like Arctic ice. He was built like the side of a barn, and aggression oozed from him.

'I ain't seen you around before,' he declared. 'I'm Charlie Barrett. I own the Circle B ranch. My son, Shep, was jailed last night, and the sheriff rode into my place in the middle of the night to tell me Shep was dead. Buck Allen said something about Shep trying to bust out of the jail through the ceiling of a cell, and ended up falling three storeys to the street. You tell me what really happened.'

'I became a deputy only this morning,' Chet replied. 'I heard what you were told. I don't know the facts of the incident. All I do know is that your son and Billy Redfern were caught threatening Mrs Hallam, the wife of the missing sheriff, in her shack, and they were jailed for questioning.'

'The hell you say. And my guess is that you're Hallam's son from Texas.' Barrett swung his right fist, taking Chet by surprise. His solid knuckles caught Chet on the chin and sent him over backwards, his senses reeling.

Chet drew his gun as his shoulders hit the ground and, despite the blackness of unconsciousness lurking in the periphery of his whirling brain, he cocked the weapon and covered Barrett.

'Back off,' he rapped. 'Hold your horses. Don't jump the gun, Barrett.'

Barrett ignored the command and reached for his holstered gun. Chet waited until the last possible moment, and fired a single shot as Barrett cleared leather. The crash of the shot thundered in the close confines of the barn. Echoes fled. Barrett twisted sideways, blood leaking from his right shoulder. He fell stiffly, like a tree blown down in a gale, and hit the ground with his face and lay unmoving. . . .

FOUR

Chet scrambled to his feet, his ears ringing from the detonation of the shot. The four cowboys were frozen in shock, their mouths agape. Chet covered them with his pistol.

'I guess you saw what happened,' Chet rasped.

One of the men, older than the others, came out of a stall. He was not tall but built like a beer barrel, his shoulders wider than normal, and his arms were long, heavily muscled. His red shirt was straining around his torso. His large head seemed too heavy for his bull neck, and he was not handsome. His features looked as if they were chiselled from rock. His eyes were well back in wrinkled sockets.

'I saw it,' he grated, 'but I don't believe it. I'm Buster Hackett, ramrod at Circle B. The boss pulled his gun on you without warning. So what gives? I haven't seen you around before. You're a stranger. Why did Charlie draw on you? He's not a violent man. Does he know you from somewhere?'

'We never set eyes on each other until I walked in that door,' Chet said. 'He spoke of his son. My law

59

badge seemed to set him off. What's he got against the local law?'

'He's a firm believer in the law – ask anyone around here. We came in with the boss this morning because Shep died in the night. That's why Charlie was all fired up. Shep was his only son.'

'That ain't any reason for him to try and shoot me. You'd better get him to the doctor before he bleeds to death. I'll report this to the sheriff.'

The cowboys picked up Barrett, who was semi-conscious and groaning, and carried him away. Chet turned to leave, but saw a man standing in the doorway of a small office just inside the stable, holding a shotgun in his hands. Chet returned his pistol to its holster and walked across to the office. The man was tall and lean, his weathered face showing suspicion, although he relaxed a little when he saw the law star on Chet's shirt.

'What in hell was that all about?' he demanded. 'I saw Charlie Barrett draw on you. I know you got into town yesterday. I saw a strange horse in one of the stalls. And today you're wearing a deputy sheriff star. Are you a friend of Buck Allen?'

'What's your name?' Chet countered.

'I'm Tom Lambert. I run this place for Matt Lomax. Who are you?'

'I'm Chet Hallam.'

'So you're related to Arch Hallam.'

'He's my father.'

'And you'll be brother to Arnie Mayhew, huh?'

'Arnie is my stepbrother. You must have known my

60

father well. He was the sheriff here for five years.'

Lambert nodded. 'I knew him well. I can't understand why he walked out like he did. He came in here for his horse the last time I saw him; said he was gonna take a ride out to Matt Sherman's ranch – something to do with rustling. He seemed quite normal, not at all like a man who was not coming back.'

'I'm here to find out what happened to him. Is there anything you can tell me that might help?'

'I've been in this business more than thirty years, and the first thing I learned was to keep my eyes open and my mouth shut.' Lambert shook his head. 'I've always stuck to that rule, and I ain't likely to change my mind about it now.'

'OK.' Chet reached into his pocket and produced a silver dollar. 'That will keep my horse in here for a few days. I'll drop by later and we'll talk some more.'

'I give the law department a special deal on their horseflesh. You can have the same deal.'

Chet turned away, and then paused. 'What colour horse did my father ride?' he asked.

'It was a chestnut. I ain't seen it around since he rode out on it and didn't come back.' Lambert turned abruptly and went inside his office.

Chet left the barn. He glanced around the street. There were folks moving around now, attracted by the shot that had been fired. A small crowd was following the cowboys carrying Charlie Barrett to the doctor's office. Sol Kennedy was standing outside the batwings of the saloon. He made no attempt to confront Hackett and the party from the Circle B. Chet crossed to where Kennedy was standing.

'Who shot Charlie Barrett?' Kennedy demanded.

Chet explained the incident, and Kennedy shrugged.

'That'll teach the local folks how many beans make five,' he said in a sombre tone. 'I could have told them about the way you worked down in Texas, but they wanted you as a deputy as soon as they learned you'd been in the Rangers and Arch Hallam is your father. They expect you to attract all the bad men in the county out into the open so one good shooting match will clear away the trouble. But it doesn't work like that, huh? You're not interested in making war on our undesirables. You're only interested in one thing – your father's disappearance. I reckon there will be some grim faces around here when you get into your stride.'

Chet shook his head. 'I don't know what you're talking about,' he said. 'The sheriff is coming along the street. Tell him what happened in the stable, will you?'

Kennedy laughed: a low, bitter sound. 'Oh, I'll tell him,' he said. 'Who are you going to shoot now?'

'Anyone who wants to trade lead with me,' Chet replied, and walked into the alley beside the saloon. He went through it to the back lot, walked to the Lomax house beyond the stage depot, and knocked on the door.

Annie Lomax answered. She gazed at Chet's set face for a moment before inviting him in. She was sedately dressed in a long blue skirt and a white blouse, her hair fixed in a neat bun at the back of her head. Her eyes showed anxiety.

'Is Arnie in?' he asked.

'He's waiting for you to call,' she replied. 'He's had a change of mind since last evening. He realizes that he's got to get along with you.'

'That sounds like your influence at work.' Chet removed his hat and stepped across the threshold.

Annie led him into a room on the left, and he saw Arnie sitting in an easy chair, reading a newspaper. His stepbrother looked up and threw aside the paper.

'It's about time you showed up,' he said in a non-committal tone.

'I can understand why you dislike my father,' Chet observed, 'but do you hate your mother for marrying my father?'

'I need to see this trouble cleared up quickly,' Arnie said. 'I've made a good life for myself around here, but I can't get on with it until the law has done what it gets paid for. I heard you got yourself a law star. I was expecting it. Now you'll start digging around for the bad men, and there'll be hell to pay. There's no telling how far you'll go, and I want something left when it's over. So I'll work with you, despite my personal feelings.'

'That's a big change of heart,' Chet observed.

'Do you want to work with me or don't you?' Irritation sounded in Arnie's tone. 'I've got an idea that might pull the Frazee gang out into the open and give you the chance to shoot the hell out of them.'

'I'm listening.' Chet sat down and gazed intently at

Arnie. 'What have you come up with?'

'I've had trouble with the gang for some weeks now. Whenever I take a coach out I can expect to see some of the bad men somewhere along the trail. They only hold up the coach when there is a strong box aboard. It's like they know which coach to stop. But where do they get their information from? I've given it a lot of thought, and it beats me.'

'Don't worry about that if you've got an idea how to lure the gang out into the open,' Chet told him.

'I've talked to Lomax about putting a strong box aboard the coach, filled with rocks so there's no danger of losing any dough should something go wrong, and you and a posse could be trailing the coach, ready to strike when the gang shows up.'

'It could work,' Chet said. 'But if the gang is getting prior information about your shipments then it'll know that your special strong box is worthless.'

'I've thought of that. We'll have to bring the bank into the scheme, and they can give us a false shipping order. It will be a bigger shipment than usual, and should tempt the gang to attack.'

'We've got nothing to lose,' Chet opined. 'I'll talk it over with the sheriff.'

'I don't want too many folks knowing about this,' Arnie said firmly. 'There's a leak somewhere in the system, and we don't know where it is.'

'There are only two places it could be – the bank, where the money comes from, or the stage line that carries the shipment. It should be simple to work out where the leak is.'

'I've got some more thinking to do on the idea. It's still got some rough edges. But are you willing to go along with it?'

'That goes without saying.' Chet nodded. 'You work out the details, let me know, and I'll have a posse ready to close the trap when you set it.'

'That's settled then. I'll start laying the plan. I'll go along to the bank shortly and talk to John Hoyt. I don't think there'll be any problems with him. He's already lost money to Frazee and his bunch. The bank has put up a thousand dollars for anyone who can provide information that will lead to the capture of the gang.'

'I'll talk to the sheriff. He'll have to know about this. But before I go, can you tell me anything about my father's trouble? He must have been up to his neck in something big enough to make him up stakes and pull out. He was never a quitter!'

'Like I told you last evening, I didn't see much of him around town. But I heard talk, and he was getting it in the neck from all sides. In fact I felt sorry for him. He was doing his best, but he was the only man in town who didn't know he hadn't a chance of beating the set-up.'

'What set-up?'

'If I knew that I'd pass the word to the law. When I marry Annie in September I'll take over running the stage line and freighting business, and I won't want a gang of robbers on my doorstep. And if we beat Frazee and knock him out of the picture perhaps your father will show up again.'

'Do you think he's still alive?' Chet demanded.

'There's no evidence that he was removed and killed.' Arnie shrugged. 'I guess only time will tell.'

Chet was fired up when he left Arnie, although he was aware that optimism should not be permitted to discolour his mind. He sensed that his father was dead, and all he could hope to do was get the men responsible. He saw his mother emerge from the hotel and walk along the boardwalk. She turned into the general store, and Chet followed her. The situation being what it was, he was afraid that someone would make another try against a defenceless woman. He could not begin to imagine what Shep Barrett and Billy Redfern had wanted from his mother the previous evening.

He entered the store and remained in the background. His mother was talking animatedly with Lucy Johnson, and he wondered why Joe Hoyt, the banker's son, would hold up a girl for money. He had the feeling that something was not quite right with that situation, and watched Lucy intently for some minutes. She was wearing a long white dust coat and presented a pleasant picture, with her hair long about her shoulders. But he thought she looked taut, stressed, and thought it might pay dividends if he got firm with her. She might tell the truth about what she was really doing in a dark alley with Joe Hoyt.

There were two other women waiting by the counter, and his mother remained chatting with Lucy. The waiting women were served and departed. Mrs Hallam looked around, saw Chet, and came over to him. She was animated for the first time since his arrival. Her eyes were bright and her voice had lost its monotone of shock.

'Hi, Chet,' she greeted. 'I'm glad you're here. I've been talking to Lucy, and heard what happened to her last evening. Come and talk to her. I reckon she could do with some help, although she won't ask for it.'

'I got the impression she didn't need help. She refused to talk to the sheriff about what happened – didn't want anyone to know that Hoyt had held her up, although she did mention to me that he had asked her for money.'

'You shouldn't take no for an answer,' said Mrs Hallam, grasping his arm and leading him to the counter where Lucy was standing. 'Lucy, tell Chet the truth about what happened to you. He's working for the local law now, and I know you can trust him.'

Lucy shook her head, her expression changing. Her smile vanished and was replaced by fear.

'There's nothing to tell,' she said, 'and I'd like to forget about what happened, if you don't mind.'

'After the incident I had the feeling you were hiding something,' Chet said, 'and if that's true then the best thing you can do is bring it out into the open.'

'Yes, Lucy,' Mrs Hallam said. 'It's the only way you can be sure that nothing else will happen to you.'

'You're a fine one to talk,' replied Lucy harshly. 'You haven't told anyone what happened to your husband. Why are you keeping silent?'

Chet frowned. His mother shook her head and

turned away; hurried out of the store, leaving Chet gazing after her in amazement. He scrutinized Lucy, who had put a hand to her mouth and looked as if she could have bitten off her tongue.

'What gives, Lucy?' he demanded. 'What am I missing? If you know anything at all about what's going on then you've got to speak up. It's your civic duty to help the law if you can, and it's against the law to remain silent if you do know something.'

'It's not for me to say anything. Please don't ask me. I've seen what happened to some of the local men who tried to help the law, and I don't want that to happen to me.'

'I'll come back to you shortly,' Chet said. 'I'd better see if my mother is all right.'

He left the store and looked around. Mrs Hallam was just disappearing into the hotel, and he hurried after her. He found her standing at the reception desk with Ellen Whiteside, who had an arm around Mrs Hallam's shoulders and was talking soothingly.

'What was that all about in the store, Ma?' Chet demanded, going to her side. 'I had the feeling you were holding out on me when we first talked. You said you knew nothing about anything. But that's not true, is it? We'd better have another chat, and this time you'll have to level with me. It's the only way to settle this trouble.'

Mrs Hallam shook her head emphatically and remained silent. Chet sighed, trying to control his impatience.

'You can't go on like this, Ma,' he persisted. 'I

need to know things. Pa disappeared, and naturally I'm thinking he's dead. But now I'm not so sure. I've got the feeling you could clear up the mystery, but you've buttoned your lip. So what gives?'

'If you'd been living here all the time, like the rest of us, you wouldn't need to ask questions about what's going on.' Mrs Hallam's lips barely moved and her voice was low and harsh. 'No one around town will say anything. You can ask all you like, but they're all too scared to talk. That's why your father isn't here today. He couldn't get anyone to back him when he was really up against it.'

'You're saying now that something is wrong, so why not give me the details? Don't you want to know what happened to Pa? He's your husband, for God's sake!'

She began to cry, and Ellen turned away with her arm around the older woman's shoulders, glancing at Chet with disapproval in her gaze.

'Come and have a cup of coffee, Mrs Hallam,' Ellen said, 'and you'll feel much better. You don't have to answer any questions if you don't want to.' She looked at Chet as she led his mother into the office. 'Leave her with me for a spell, and talk to her again later.'

Chet shook his head and hurried back to the store. A voice hailed him and he turned quickly to see Sol Kennedy coming along the boardwalk. The big deputy beckoned to him, and Chet shook his head impatiently.

'We need a charge against Billy Redfern if we're

gonna hold him any longer,' Kennedy said. 'Have you found out what he and Shep Barrett were doing at your mother's shack?'

'I'm working on that angle,' Chet replied, 'but at the moment no one is talking about anything.'

'Tell me something I don't know.' Kennedy shook his head. 'We need some proof about something, and quick. Get your teeth into someone and shake evidence out of him. Then we can do our job. By the way, the sheriff turned Joe Hoyt loose a moment ago. He's practically helpless with the busted jaw you gave him, and we know that Lucy Johnson won't give evidence against him, not in a hundred years.'

'Did you tell the sheriff about Charlie Barrett?' Chet asked.

'Yeah. He'll be taken into custody when his shoulder has been attended to. He's badly shook up about his son, and the sheriff reckons to hold him until he gets over the shock.'

Chet turned away and went on to the store. Lucy was no longer behind the counter, and he approached the older woman there in the girl's place.

'Where's Lucy?' he demanded. 'I was in here talking to her a couple of minutes ago.'

'So you're the new deputy who's upsetting everyone, huh? I'm Lucy's mother, and she's badly troubled.'

'I got her out of a nasty situation last night,' Chet retorted, 'and I broke Joe Hoyt's jaw in doing so. My only intention is to prevent the same sort of thing happening again, to Lucy or any other woman. So get Lucy out here and I'll talk to her.'

'You can't help Lucy. You'll only make matters worse if you persist. Give her a break. Leave her alone.'

'Where is she?' Chet's tone roughened as his patience fled. 'I'm going to talk to her whether she likes it or not. I have reason to believe she's withholding evidence about a misdemeanour committed in her presence. I've just heard that Joe Hoyt has been released from jail because there's no charge against him. If I were you I'd be concerned to know he is on the prowl again.'

'She's not here at the moment.' Mrs Johnson ignored Chet's warning. 'I've sent her out to deliver supplies to one of our customers.'

'She could be in danger alone the street. If you care anything at all about her safety you'll tell me where she's gone.'

Mrs Johnson shook her head. 'We'll look after our own,' she rapped, and turned to serve a woman who came to the counter.

'Where's Lucy's father?' Chet demanded. 'I need to have a few words with him.'

'He passed me on the sidewalk,' the customer said. 'He looked to be in a real bad mood, and he's carrying a shotgun.'

Chet ran from the store and looked around the street. He saw Lucy in the vicinity of the saloon, and a tall, thin man wearing an apron was behind her, a double-barrelled shotgun in his hands. Chet ran toward them. His feet pounded the boardwalk and, as

71

he closed the distance between them, the man with the gun glanced over his shoulder and then turned to face him, pulling back the hammers on his gun.

Lucy turned as her father called a challenge, and she ran back the several paces between them and put a hand on the shotgun, pushing the fearsome muzzles down until they pointed at the boardwalk.

'He's on my side, Pa,' she said urgently. 'He's the one who helped me against Joe Hoyt last evening.'

'So you do know I'm on your side,' Chet said. 'So why aren't you helping me?' He looked into Johnson's eyes. 'And what kind of a fool are you, coming on the street with a loaded shotgun? Who are you planning to shoot?'

'Anyone who tries to cause more trouble for my daughter,' Johnson said.

'Then you'd better keep your eyes open for Joe Hoyt,' Chet said softly. 'The sheriff has just released him from jail.'

Johnson's expression changed instantly, and he twisted around to survey the street. Chet turned as well; saw Joe Hoyt coming across the street towards them and called to Lucy to get off the street. Chet kept his eyes on Hoyt, who had a bandage around his lower face. When he saw Hoyt lift a pistol from his holster, he set his own hand in motion.

Hoyt halted as he made his draw. Chet cleared leather, and found the time to push Johnson to one side, using his left hand. Hoyt levelled his gun; his target was Chet. Then the shooting started. . . .

FIVE

Hoyt got off the first shot. Chet heard the slug crackle by his right ear. He dropped to one knee and triggered his pistol, aiming for Hoyt's right thigh. The bullet struck, and Hoyt dropped to his hands and knees, losing his grip on his gun. His fingers scrabbled in the dust as he tried to locate the weapon. Chet fired again, and the discarded gun jumped and skittered away out of Hoyt's reach.

Chet went forward to where Hoyt was down. Hoyt's right hand was in his jacket pocket, and Chet saw the gleam of sunlight on metal as the hand reappeared. He stepped forward a quick pace and kicked out as Hoyt tried to bring a hideout gun to bear. The toe of Chet's boot connected with Hoyt's hand and a .41 derringer flew out of his fingers. Chet swung his pistol and slammed the barrel against Hoyt's head. Hoyt collapsed in the dust and lay unmoving.

Chet glanced around. Lucy was peering at him from the doorway of a butcher's shop. Her father was standing motionless on the spot where Chet had pushed him, still gripping his shotgun but now looking foolish. Chet saw Kennedy coming fast along the sidewalk, gun in hand, and the big deputy was breathless when he reached Chet's side. Gun echoes were fading into the distance.

'What the hell happened?' Kennedy demanded.

Chet ignored the question. 'Take Hoyt and stick him back in a cell. I'll charge him with attempted murder.'

'Have you got any witnesses?' Kennedy demanded.

'Didn't you see what happened?' Chet countered.

'No. I was in the gun shop when I heard the shooting. I walked across the street with Hoyt when the sheriff turned him loose and left him at the door of the gun shop.'

'Talk to Johnson,' Chet said sharply. 'He must have seen the whole thing. And keep Hoyt behind bars after this. If he comes for me again I'll shoot him dead centre.'

'I'll take him to see Doc Fletcher first.'

'Where's the sheriff?' Chet demanded. 'Doesn't he stick his nose out of the office when he hears shooting on the street?'

'He rode out of town ten minutes ago.' Kennedy grimaced. 'He's got to make a couple of calls on the range.'

Chet went to Johnson. The store owner was pale-faced. It was likely his first close contact with a shooting. He was gripping his shotgun with both hands, his knuckles white under the pressure, and Chet had to slap his shoulder before animation flowed through him again.

'Where's Lucy?' Johnson asked, shaking his head. He saw Hoyt lying in the dust and a tremor ran through his lean body. 'Have you killed him?' he demanded. He saw Kennedy begin to drag Hoyt upright and breath escaped him in a long sigh. 'He's not dead!' he gasped. 'Why didn't you kill him when you had the chance?'

'I don't shoot men for the fun of it,' Chet replied. 'I fired only to disarm him. Go back to the store and put your shotgun away.'

'Lucy?' Johnson repeated.

'She's safe. I want to talk to her now. I'll bring her back to the store when I get through with her.'

He pushed Johnson in the back to get him moving, and the man went obediently along the sidewalk, like a sleepwalker, accompanied by Kennedy. Folk were appearing on the street, attracted by the shooting. Chet went to where Lucy was standing in the shop doorway. She was shocked; hands to her face, eyes wide and blank.

'I should have warned you to watch out for Hoyt,' she said in a trembling tone.

'Why didn't you?' Chet countered. 'I gave you a chance to say something. But perhaps you'll be more forthcoming now. Come with me. We'll get a cup of coffee, and you can tell me about your problems.'

She shook her head mutely. Chet slid his left hand under her arm and drew her forward into motion. She tried to draw back at first, but his insistent hand kept her moving, and they went along the sidewalk to the hotel, followed by a little knot of curious towns-men.

At the hotel, Ellen Whiteside provided two cups of coffee, and Chet seated Lucy at a corner table in the dining room. He sat down opposite her, remaining silent. He heard Lucy's teeth click against the coffee cup as she drank some of its contents. A little colour began to seep back into her pale features, and she blinked rapidly as she came slowly out of her shock.

'Is my father all right?' she asked. She did not meet his gaze but looked steadily into her cup.

'He's gone back to the store. I'll take you there when we've had a chat.' He saw her expression change. She opened her mouth to speak but closed it again. 'You're aware now that you should have told me whatever it is you know about Joe Hoyt,' Chet persisted. 'He wouldn't have been turned loose this morning if you'd made a charge against him – explained exactly what happened last evening, and there wouldn't have been shooting on the street this morning. It was a good lesson to learn. Folks could have been caught in that flying lead. Supposing your father had been killed! You didn't think of that before, but it must be in your mind now.'

'I'm sorry,' she muttered. 'I am truly sorry. Hoyt has been taking money from us for months now – every week he wants a percentage of our takings, for which we receive protection.' She laughed harshly. 'At first we refused, but he, Billy Redfern and Shep Barrett were in it together, and they threatened us until we gave in. Hoyt caught me out one evening and took me into the stable; held a knife against my throat and threatened to kill me if we didn't pay up. They are taking money off most of the businesses in town.'

'Shep Barrett died escaping from the jail last night,' Chet told her. 'He would still be alive if you had spoken of this yesterday. So I'll need a statement from you now, giving details of everything that's happened in connection with Hoyt's plan to get money from your business. Will you do that?'

'What about the threats Hoyt made?' she demanded. She was breathing raggedly, as if she could not get sufficient air into her lungs.

'Hoyt and Redfern will be behind bars for a long time to come, and Barrett is dead. Tell me the names of everyone else who was in the racket to extort money from the townsfolk.'

'That nasty man, Waco Sim, was sometimes with Hoyt when I was accosted. I'm certain he knew what was going on, even if he wasn't actively involved.'

'Sim, huh?' Chet's eyes gleamed. 'That's interesting. I was wondering why he shot at me! Can you name others who were paying Hoyt for so-called protection?'

Lucy nodded. Her tone had changed, suggesting that she was no longer reluctant to tell what she knew. The act of making the effort to talk about her problem had evidently loosened her tongue.

'Beth Howard owns the dress shop. She's my friend. She told me Hoyt was taking regular payments from her. Nobody dared go against Hoyt.

77

Some townsmen were beaten when they refused to pay, and going to the law was not a good idea. Hoyt and the others proved they could get to anyone before the law could intervene.'

'Not any more,' Chet said firmly. 'You must make a statement now, Lucy, and then I'll approach folks around town and get statements from those caught up in this crooked scheme. That will put an end to it.'

She nodded, but did not seem happy to fall in with his wishes. Chet drank his coffee and stood up, chair scraping on the wooden floor. Lucy arose, and he escorted her out to the street. She looked around as if expecting to be assaulted without warning. Chet led her across the street and they entered the building opposite. Pete Sayer let them into the law department. Kennedy was sitting at the desk, and he grinned when he saw Lucy.

'Is she going to make a statement?' Kennedy demanded. 'Her father wouldn't say anything.'

'You sound as if you know what's been going on,' Chet countered. He pulled a chair to the side of the desk and Lucy sat down.

'I had a suspicion,' Kennedy admitted, 'but no one was talking, and there's nothing we can do without statements.'

'Take a statement from Lucy. I want to talk to Billy Redfern.'

Sayer picked up the cell keys and led the way into the cell block. Chet looked at the cell where Barrett had been the night before, and shook his head when he saw where part of the ceiling had been pulled down during the abortive escape attempt.

'That was a bad business,' Sayer commented. 'There's going be hell about it. Charlie Barrett attacked you, and it didn't help matters that you plugged him.'

'I'm sorry,' Chet retorted. 'I didn't realize I should have let him shoot me!'

Sayer grinned. 'As far as I'm concerned, the more like him around here you shoot the better,' he replied. 'But I prefer them as prisoners. They keep me in a job.' He paused at a cell, and Chet saw Redfern inside, sitting on a bunk, head in his hands. 'Do you want the door unlocked?' Sayer demanded.

Chet nodded. Sayer unlocked the cell door and departed. Chet stepped into the cell. Redfern did not move. He was staring at the floor, elbows on his knees and hands cupped to support his head. He was big – over six feet, brown-haired and bearded. Chet could imagine how he would scare women.

'Redfern,' he rapped. 'Snap out of it. You've got some talking to do.'

Redfern looked up at him but did not move. After several moments he turned his gaze back to the floor.

'Pay attention,' Chet said sharply. 'Tell me about the protection racket you've been running with Joe Hoyt and Shep Barrett.'

'I don't know what you're talking about.' Redfern stirred, leaned back on the bunk until his shoulders touched the bars at his back. 'When are you gonna turn me loose?' he demanded. 'I wasn't doing anything at the Hallam shack. I was outside. It was Redfern went in to see the woman.'

'That woman is my mother.' Chet held down his anger. 'So what was Barrett's intention? He's not here now to explain, so it rests with you to tell what you know.'

'I don't know what was in his mind. We were in the saloon together, and he said he had to make a call. I just went along with him.'

'I've got a witness who has stated that you, Hoyt and Barrett were taking money off her father and other folks in town. You'll have to answer a charge that will be brought against you. If you have any sense at all you'll tell me what was going on, and maybe you'll get a lighter sentence if I can tell the court you've been helpful to the law.'

'No dice! I've got nothing to say. I've told you I know nothing about that business, and you ain't gonna get the chance to twist anything I say into a confession of guilt. Let me out of here. I've got things to do.'

'Like scaring women and taking their money, huh? OK, have it your way. I've given you a chance to help yourself, but if you're too stupid to take it then I'll gather evidence against you and put you before the court. Don't say you haven't been warned. The evidence I've heard so far will get you a cell in the big prison for at least five years.'

Chet left the cell and went back into the office. Sayer went immediately to lock the door of Redfern's cell. Kennedy was taking down Lucy's statement, and

Chet remained in the background, listening. The girl had recovered her poise now and eagerness sounded in her voice. When she had completed and signed her statement she sighed with relief and leaned back in her chair, smiling wanly at Chet.

'That's all I can tell you,' she said. 'I hope it will help.'

'That was good,' he told her. 'It's just what we needed! All I want you to do now is accompany me to see some of the folks you say were also being robbed and help me convince them to give evidence against Hoyt. Then you'll be finished, and we can start cleaning up.'

'Shall we be safe from those men?' she asked.

'Don't worry about them. Everyone involved will be behind bars before they know what's happening.'

Lucy did not reply, but her expression showed that she was not fully convinced by his words. He turned to Kennedy.

'I'll try and get some of the folks involved to come in and make statements,' he said. 'The sooner I get this wrapped up the sooner I can get down to the business I'm really interested in – my father's disappearance. One thing is bothering me, Kennedy. How come you or the sheriff didn't notice what was going on around here? Folk were being shaken down, threatened, and beaten up in some cases, but nobody took any action.'

'What are you trying to say?' Kennedy demanded. 'We didn't have the time to go nosing around town for small-time crooks. Maybe that was why your father ran out – it got too hot for him.'

'Are you suggesting he knew about this business?'

'I ain't suggesting anything. I'm only asking questions, the same as you.'

Chet shook his head. 'Come on, Lucy, let's get it done.'

'Do I have to confront the folks I know?' she demanded. 'They told me in confidence about this. I'd rather not be dragged into the unpleasantness that will be stirred up. You could tell them I've made a statement about my own experience, and that you are asking around because it's obvious my family isn't the only victim.'

Chet studied her face for some moments. He sighed heavily. 'OK, I'll play it your way. You've been a great help by telling me what happened to you. In a case like this it's usually harder for someone to be the first to make a statement. I guess I can carry on from here. I'll see you to the store, and you'd better remain close to home until after I've set the ball rolling.'

She nodded, her face showing relief. Chet escorted her out of the building and they crossed the street to the store. He entered with her, and her father was standing behind the counter with her mother, talking to several townsmen clustered together and listening intently to what Johnson was saying. The storekeeper fell silent when he saw Chet, and came hurrying around the counter to confront Lucy.

'What have you done, Lucy?' he demanded. 'If

you've spilled that can of beans then there'll be hell to pay. We'll be finished around here.'

'Listen to me,' Chet said. 'Lucy has made a statement about what happened to her last evening when she was accosted by Joe Hoyt. She is required by law to do so, and that is all she's done. Now give her a break. I'll take action on what I've learned about a certain problem, and if I come to any of you men now present I shall expect you to be as open and forthcoming as Lucy has been. The only way to settle this trouble is to be honest and bring the facts into the open.'

Johnson shook his head. 'It won't be that easy,' he said. 'Folks could get hurt before you take the bull by the horns.'

'You're in this situation because you didn't get together and make a firm stand against the men involved,' Chet insisted. 'Joe Hoyt is in jail and so is Redfern. If you know the names of anyone else involved in the crooked business then tell me and I'll jail them.'

He paused, but no one spoke.

'Think it over,' he told them. 'This is your chance to put a stop to these hard cases.'

He left the store and went along to the hotel. Ellen Whiteside was at the reception desk. She was looking worried, and Chet guessed she was not the only one in town now faced with a big problem.

'I know about the extortion racket that's going on in town,' he told her. 'Joe Hoyt and his friends are handling it. Lucy Johnson has made a statement about it, and other folk are beginning to see their way clear to reporting it. It would be to your advantage to add your name to the list of victims, Ellen. I guess you are involved. There'll be no danger for you and your father. Bring the business out into the open and that will put an end to it.'

She nodded but remained silent, and he could tell by her expression that she was giving some serious thought to the situation.

'I need to talk to my mother,' he went on. 'She spilled the beans about the extortion, and I'm afraid she's badly upset. Is she in her room?'

'She went up the stairs, so I guess that's where she is.'

He turned to the stairs, but Ellen called to him. When he turned to face her she sighed heavily.

'I'll make a statement,' she said.

He smiled. 'That's good. I'll just check on my mother, and then I'll come back to you.'

He went up the stairs and knocked on the door of his mother's room. When there was no answer he tried the door. It opened, and he discovered she was not in. He turned quickly, and his boots thudded heavily on the stairs as he descended. Ellen, at the desk, looked up as he confronted her.

'Ma's not in her room,' Chet said heavily. 'Are you sure she went up to it?'

'She did. She was in a hurry, and didn't stop when I called her name. She hasn't come down again, so she must have used the back stairs if she's left the hotel.'

84

Chet ran out of the hotel and hurried into the alley at the side. He ran along its length to the back lot and looked around. There was no sign of his mother. He heaved a sigh, and then his gaze alighted on the stage depot. He thought instantly of Arnie, and headed towards the Lomax house. As he reached the front door it opened and Annie appeared. She halted at the sight of him.

'If you're here to see Arnie you're out of luck,' she said. 'He went to see the doctor earlier, and he isn't back yet.'

'It's my mother,' he replied, and told her what had happened.

Annie's face changed expression. 'She didn't come here,' she said. 'And there aren't many places she could go to for help.'

'Has she any friends in town?' he asked.

'None I know! We haven't been very friendly with your family because of Arnie's attitude. It was not what I wanted, but you know Arnie better than me, and when he's made up his mind to something nothing will change it.'

Chet shook his head and took his leave. He went back to Main Street and walked the length of it, looking into the establishments along the way. There was no sign of his mother, and he ended up entering the law office. His mind was in turmoil. His father had disappeared mysteriously and now his mother had gone. He wondered what had triggered her into action. She had brought the protection racket into the open. He wondered if someone had abducted her. Barrett and Redfern had been at her shack the previous night, and Redfern obviously knew something. His attitude earlier had suggested that he was holding something back.

Pete Sayer admitted him to the law office. Kennedy was not there. Sayer returned to the desk and sat down to resume reading a newspaper.

'I want to talk to Redfern again,' Chet said. 'If he knows anything about what's going on, now is the time to get it out of him.'

'No rough stuff,' Sayer said quickly. 'I won't stand for that.'

'Barrett and Redfern saw my mother last night, and they were threatening her about something. Now she's disappeared, and if Redfern does know anything then he'll talk. So open his cell door, and don't get in my way.'

'If it's about your mother then I'll help you make him talk,' Sayer responded. He picked up the cell keys. 'Let's get to it, huh?'

They went through to the cells. Sayer led the way to Redfern's cell, and then uttered an exclamation and hurriedly unlocked the door. Chet looked over the jailer's shoulder and saw Redfern sagging at the window, lolling on a belt that was around his neck and looped through the window bars. . . .

SIX

Sayer lunged into the cell and hurled himself at the motionless figure. Chet was right behind him. They grabbed Redfern and lifted him to ease the pressure of the belt around his neck. Redfern's face was blue, contorted, his mouth agape, tongue protruding. Chet supported the man's dead weight while Sayer fumbled with the belt buckle. There was a deadly silence in the cell. Sayer was gasping for breath, shocked by the situation. He unfastened the belt and they placed Redfern on the bunk. Sayer pressed an ear against Redfern's chest. His gaze lifted to Chet's taut face as he shook his head slowly and straightened.

'Heart's stopped. He's dead.' Sayer sat down suddenly on a corner of the bunk as if his legs had refused to support him. 'He was OK fifteen minutes ago,' he continued. 'I knew he was shocked by Barrett's death, but I didn't expect this.'

'You'd better fetch the doctor,' Chet said. 'I'll stay here.'

Sayer got to his feet and scurried from the cell. Chet could hear his boots thudding on the stairs. Shock was clouding his thought processes. What was going on behind the scenes in this apparently quiet town? He went into the law office, sat down at the desk, and had to make an effort to get his thoughts moving again.

He needed to talk to Joe Hoyt, and there was Charlie Barrett in the background. He needed to cut through the barrier of silence. But his mother had to be his first priority. She must have been badly worried about something to feel compelled to flee.

When Sayer came back into the office he was followed by a short, fleshy man carrying a medical bag. The doctor was in his middle forties, wearing a grey store suit, and his expression showed the effects of the traumas of his professional life.

'This is Doc Fletcher,' Sayer announced. 'Chet Hallam, Doc.'

Chet got to his feet and shook hands. 'Hi, Doc,' he greeted. 'Redfern hanged himself in his cell. Your visit is just a matter of routine.'

'I'm glad to meet you,' Fletcher replied in a low-pitched voice. 'I've been saying for a long time that we needed some new blood in this office, and I know you've got to shoot people if they won't behave, but I'm being run off my feet since you started working for the law.'

'That's the way it goes.' Chet grimaced. 'Where have you got Joe Hoyt and Charlie Barrett, Doc? I need to speak to the pair of them.'

'They're not fit to leave my place at the moment,' Fletcher said. 'I've got a couple of rooms fitted up as a makeshift hospital, and they'll be kept there until they are fit to join you here. But call in at any time to see them. My wife is always on hand, and she is a trained nurse. Now take me to see Billy Redfern.'

'Before you go, Doc, tell me if you've being paying the men running the protection racket around here.'

'Everybody pays,' Fletcher replied. 'I've got nothing to say until you've put all the bad men out of circulation.'

'Give me their names and I'll deal with them,' Chet countered.

Fletcher eyed him for a moment, nodding his head slowly. 'You look like your father,' he said at length. 'He was a good lawman. I guess that's why he's gone. By the way, John Hoyt, the banker was in my place to see his son earlier, and he asked me to tell you on the quiet that he would like to talk to you.'

'Thanks, Doc.' Chet nodded. 'I've been meaning to get around to seeing him but I've been kept busy on other matters. I will make a point of seeing him shortly. Now I'll leave you in Pete's hands.'

Fletcher nodded and went into the cells, followed by Sayer. Chet left the office and went out to the street. He crossed at an angle, reaching the opposite sidewalk almost in front of the bank; a brick-built building next to the butcher's shop. As he walked to the bank door he heard the sound of spurs tinkling behind him and glanced over his shoulder. Buster Hackett, the Circle B ramrod, was hurrying to catch up with him.

'Got a minute?' Hackett called.

'All the time in the world, if you've got something worthwhile to tell me,' Chet replied.

Hackett smiled, but his face was set in a serious expression. 'Charlie Barrett wants to see you,' he said.

'I had a feeling he might ask for me. I've got him on my list of men to see, and I'll get around to him sometime today.'

'It's kind of urgent for Charlie. Can you move him up your list?'

'I'll visit him after I've called in here.' Chet reached out for the door of the bank.

Hackett nodded and turned away. Chet watched him for a moment, and then entered the bank.

A tall, thin man in his fifties was standing in front of the teller's cage, chatting with the clerk behind the grille. He was smartly dressed in a town suit, white shirt, and had a string tie at his throat. Chet guessed this was the banker. An office door to the right was open, and Chet got a glimpse inside. The banker straightened and turned around. He was smiling, but the smile disappeared when he saw the law star on Chet's shirt front. He eyed Chet for a moment and then nodded.

'You must be Chet Hallam,' he said. 'You look a lot like your father. I'm John Hoyt. Did you get my message that I wanted to talk to you?'

'That's why I'm here. Why didn't you deliver the message in person?'

'I was in a hurry. I needed to see my son, and I had to get back here for business.'

'You don't look very busy at the moment,' Chet observed.

'Please step into my office.' Hoyt moved toward the open office door and Chet followed him. Hoyt entered and then turned and, when Chet entered the office, Hoyt closed the door. He waved to a seat in front of his desk and went to sit down behind it. He leaned his elbows on the desk and craned forward.

'What do you want with me?' Chet demanded.

'You've given my son Joseph a load of trouble since you hit town,' Hoyt said.

'Nothing he didn't ask for. Do you want me to go into details?'

'What have you got against him?'

Chet explained the incident that had occurred in the alley beside the saloon, and Hoyt's expression hardened as he listened. He sighed heavily.

'I don't know where he gets his attitude from. I guess I'm to blame, letting him run wild. I should have made him toe the line and take a job here in the bank. But he got into bad company. Did Lucy Johnson make a charge against him?'

'I'm going to charge him with attempting to murder me. He drew a gun on me and started shooting. There are witnesses. I had to shoot him to put him out of action. Now he's in real trouble.'

'There's been no real harm done. You could call it quits. Joseph is going to be on his back for weeks, and he'll suffer a lot of pain. I'm an important man around here, and I could show my appreciation in different ways. For instance, I hear you're looking for a house in town. The bank has several properties on its books. You could live in one rent free for as long as you need it.'

'That sounds like a bribe. But your son is not just a wilful teenager. He's been bossing a bunch of men running a protection racket. I've got witnesses coming forward now, all eager to talk about their experience at the hands of your son and his friends. None of that can be swept under the carpet, and I can't be persuaded to change the course of the law. Your son stuck his neck out and now he's got to face the music.'

'Your father disappeared suddenly,' Hoyt said. 'He was a man who would never see reason.'

'If you know anything about his disappearance then you'd better speak up right now and tell me what you know. I'll get around later to investigating my father's last actions around town, and if I have to do it the hard way then a lot of men are going to find they're between a rock and a hard place.'

'Don't get me wrong. I don't know anything about your father.' Hoyt lifted his hands from the desk and held them up as if hoping to calm Chet. 'Have you taken into account the outlaw gang at work in the county?'

'Mitch Frazee? I've heard about that bunch, and

I'll look for them when I've cleared up this protection racket business.'

'Your father thought he could run the law by himself, but the system beat him in the end. What makes you think you can do any better?'

'I'm doing better at the moment!' Chet smiled. 'So what do you really want to see me about, apart from trying to bribe me to go easy on your son?'

'You've got hold of the wrong end of the stick. I'm not trying anything. I'm only concerned about my son.'

'And my only concern is my job. So stop wasting my time.' Chet got up and left the office despite Hoyt's attempt to keep him. He paused in the doorway, his eyes narrowing as he gazed at a woman standing in front of the teller's position. Maisie was decked out in a flowing blue dress. She was carrying a large handbag, and was in the act of placing a stack of greenbacks in front of the teller, laughing as if she hadn't a care in the world. The teller was a young man – wore glasses and a light grey suit. His blond hair was slicked down.

Chet went to Maisie's side. His right elbow nudged her and she glanced swiftly at him, her smile vanishing.

'Where did you spring from?' she demanded.

'What are you doing in here?' he countered. 'Not robbing the bank, huh?'

'If you're hunting bank robbers then you'll have to look elsewhere.' She smiled, but her eyes were cold, wary.

'Finish your business and then we'll have a chat,' Chet said.

She started to protest, thought better of it, and closed her mouth determinedly. The teller, who had been laughing easily with her, had fallen silent at the sight of Chet, and counted Maisie's cash quickly and then signed the book Maisie produced.

'See you tomorrow, Maisie,' he said, and Chet noted that a fine sheen of sweat had appeared on his forehead.

'Not if I see you first,' she joked, but her voice was flat and serious.

Chet escorted her to the door, opened it for her, and followed her out to the sidewalk.

'I've had orders from Sol Kennedy not to talk to you,' she said sharply. 'I hate the sight of him but he's taken a fancy to me, and he's a very jealous man. I wouldn't put it past him to shoot you in the back if he thought you were keen on me – which you were back in Texas.'

'I was young and foolish in those days,' Chet replied. 'Let's go along to the hotel and get a cup of coffee. I need to talk to you.'

'There's nothing I can tell you, Chet, and it wouldn't do my reputation any good to be seen in your company.'

'You don't have a choice,' he said sharply. 'Come on.' He took her arm and led her along the board-walk towards the hotel, and although she stiffened at their contact she did not resist.

'I don't want to be seen in your company,' she

94

protested. 'If Kennedy should see us together you'll have a lot more trouble on your plate. He's lost his mind over me. He's beaten up a couple of men he thought were getting too interested in me.'

'If you were concerned about my health then, aware of his temperament, why did you tell him about us down in Texas? I've got a nasty feeling you've been playing the men you know against each other. Who owns the saloon where you're working?'

'Bull Wainwright and he's a nasty type where nosey lawmen are concerned.'

'So what's new? You couldn't pick a decent man if you tried. There's one thing bothering me, Maisie. You left Texas for health reasons after the big show-down. How come you finished up here; the place my folks came to when they left Texas? That's kind of a big coincidence in my book.'

She looked at him – a sideways glance – her eyes filled with a fleeting emotion that showed her true feelings before it disappeared. She was a woman who was suddenly seeing her world collapsing around her.

'I can't answer that question without incriminating myself, Chet. I knew from the moment I set eyes on you that this would be a repeat of what happened in Texas, so I'll get out of town on the next stage, and you'll never see me again.'

'Not this time, Maisie. I took pity on you in Texas. But this time my family is involved. My father has disappeared.'

They entered the hotel and Chet spoke to Ellen Whiteside.

'I'd like two cups of coffee please, and may I use your office for a few moments? Maisie is an old friend of mine, and she has a lot to say to me.'

'I'll get the coffee for you,' Ellen said. 'Is there any word from your mother yet?'

'No. And I'm being held up by side issues that are preventing me from getting at the problems involving my family.'

He took Maisie's arm and led her into the hotel office, seated her on a chair, and sat down at the desk.

'I asked you how you managed to find your way here after leaving Texas,' he said. 'Tell me the truth, Maisie. If I catch you out in a lie you'll be sorry.'

'Let me get the next coach out, Chet, for old time's sake,' she pleaded.

'That happened the last time.' He shook his head. 'Tell me the truth, and if you are not too involved I'll let you get on the next stage out.'

She looked into his eyes, and he was surprised at the change that had come over her. She was pale-faced, her lips were dry, and she was trembling. Despair showed plainly in her gaze. She moistened her lips.

'I'll trust you, Chet,' she said in a low tone. 'You were good to me before. I don't like what's been going on around here, and I wish I'd never showed up. But I had nowhere to go, and your brother Arnie said it would be a new beginning for me if I followed him here. I wish now I'd gone in the opposite direction. Arnie is nothing like you. He's cruel. It was a

96

side of him I never saw in Texas, and when I got here and found what he was really like it was too late for me to move on.'

Chet frowned. 'What's Arnie got to do with this? Did you know him back in Texas?'

'He chased after me whenever you weren't around.' Her voice was low, intent, and quivered slightly. 'I stayed with him when I first arrived, but it didn't take him long to get his sights on Annie Lomax. She fell for him, and he fell in love with her father's business. They're getting married in September and he's taking over the business after that.'

'I can see you're telling the truth,' Chet said slowly. 'I know Arnie only too well. So he's still up to his old tricks. He's involved in running a protection racket around here.'

'I know all about it. Arnie has got a finger in several pies around here, and the way you've been tearing into Joe Hoyt and his pards has upset a lot of men.'

'What about my father? What happened to him, and who is responsible for his disappearance?'

'Chet, they'll kill me if it gets out that I've opened my mouth.' Fear sounded in her voice and her hands shook. 'You wouldn't throw me to the wolves, would you?'

'I hope you know me better than that,' he replied grimly. 'You'll have to trust me on that, Maisie. Just remember that I got you clear the last time.'

'They got rid of your father so Buck Allen and Sol

Kennedy could take over the local law.'

'Who did?'

'Mitch Frazee. The gang is hiding out at Sherman's SD ranch. They'll be pulling out when they've grabbed everything they want from around here. And there are a lot of men in town who are sticking their hands in the pot while it's still got some honey. Joe Hoyt set up his crooked business with Frazee's backing, and it would be good for you to look closer at John Hoyt's dealings.'

'Sherman's ranch is where my father was riding to on the day he disappeared,' Chet mused. 'The livery man said so – and you didn't tell me about it when you first saw me in town.' He stood up so violently his chair overturned.

'I reckon your father was killed the moment he reached Sherman's spread,' Maisie said.

'He was up against Frazee and his gang and didn't know it.' Chet considered what Maisie had said; his mind teeming with the facts, but he had no idea where to make a start on the trouble that had beaten his father. Buck Allen and Sol Kennedy were bad men, and he knew from experience that he had to clean up the law department before even considering anything else. Allen had left town, but now was a good time to confront Kennedy.

'What are you thinking, Chet?' Maisie demanded. 'You can't clean up this county without help.'

'Don't tell me what I know. You'd better start thinking about your own position. If I were in your shoes I'd catch the next stage out – to anywhere. And don't show up any place I might be in future. Have you got that?'

She nodded and got to her feet. 'It's goodbye then, Chet.' She smiled wanly. 'Take care of yourself. I hope this works out the way you want it to.'

He did not reply but stood gazing at her. She regarded him for several heart-stopping moments, and then sighed and turned away, leaving the office without a backward glance. He did not stop her. When she had gone he prepared to leave – checked his gun and slid it back into its holster. It was time to start cleaning up, and the first man he wanted in his sights was Sol Kennedy.

Chet stepped out to the sidewalk in front of the hotel and paused to look around. Maisie was walking along the boardwalk – head bent, shoulders shaking – making for the saloon. Sol Kennedy emerged from an alley across the street, his face showing jealous rage. The crooked deputy almost ran across the street to get to Maisie's side, and Chet called a warning. Maisie turned quickly, looked back at him, and caught sight of Kennedy lunging across the street with deadly intention.

Kennedy halted abruptly when he saw Chet. He glanced at Maisie, turned squarely to face Chet, and reached for his holstered gun. Chet matched him, as if one single brain controlled them. Kennedy's gun cleared leather. Chet lifted his pistol. Then the silence that lay heavily over the town was shattered by the heavy, echoing detonations of pistol shots.

Chet heard the crackle of a slug in his left ear and

dropped to his knees even as his .45 belched smoke and flame. Kennedy was triggering his second shot when Chet's bullet smashed into his chest. His legs lost their strength. He floundered like a drunken man to keep his balance and work his gun. Chet fired again, gritting his teeth as gun smoke blew back into his face.

Kennedy reeled as if he had been kicked by a mule. He let go of his gun as he dropped to his knees; saw the boards of the sidewalk coming up to smack him in the face just before oblivion overtook him. . . .

SEVEN

Chet got to his feet, mindful of the growling echoes of the shots fading away across the town. He checked his surroundings as he went forward to where Maisie was standing with her hands to her face. Kennedy was stretched out on his back, his craggy face strangely composed in death, his dead eyes staring unfocused at the sun.

'Get the next stage out, Maisie,' said Chet, holstering his gun. 'There's nothing more for you here.'

'Is he dead?' Maisie quavered.

'He's dead enough to be buried! Go on and get away before his friends find out he's cashed his chips.'

'Chet, you must go to Kennedy's house. He's got your mother locked in there!'

'What the hell!' He stared at her, shocked into immobility, his mind grappling with the news. 'My mother?' he demanded. 'How do you know? What would Kennedy want with her?'

'He was waiting all morning for the chance to grab

her. He told me earlier to go to her shack and get some clothes for her. I don't know why he wanted her.'

'Come with me!' He grasped her arm and compelled her to accompany him. 'Where did Kennedy live?'

'It's a law-house which is just past the saloon. I'll show you where it is, but I won't go in. I can't afford to be seen in your company.'

'If you want your freedom then you'll have to work for it. Make it quick, Maisie, or I'll throw the book at you.'

She turned and started along the street. Townsfolk were gathering at a safe distance from Kennedy's body, evidently expecting more action.

'Anything we can do to help?' a man demanded as Chet passed him.

'Yeah, get the undertaker to remove that body.' Chet retained a hold on Maisie's arm.

Some of the watchers followed, and more folk were coming out of the buildings. Word went around quickly that Sol Kennedy had been killed by the new deputy. Chet ignored all further questions, and the townsmen began to turn away, probably afraid of becoming involved in further action.

They passed the saloon, where a knot of men were standing outside the batwings. One of them, a very tall man, dressed in a good, expensive brown suit, reached out as Maisie passed him and grasped her arm.

'What's going on, Maisie?' he demanded.

Chet struck the hand and the man withdrew it, his face darkening with sudden anger.

'Don't hinder the law,' Chet said sharply. He continued, ignoring the muttering that followed them along the boardwalk.

'Who is the guy that put a hand on you?' Chet demanded.

'That's Bull Wainwright. He owns the saloon,' Maisie replied.

'Is he mixed up in the crookedness around here?'

'I don't know.'

'I'll find out before this is over,' Chet rapped.

'That's Kennedy's place,' Maisie said at length, as they reached a small house at the end of a row fronting the street.

Chet saw a man standing in the open doorway of the house; a short, fat individual wearing a pistol in a holster on a sagging gun belt around his fleshy waist.

'Who is he?' Chet demanded.

'Dick Masson, one of Kennedy's friends. He's probably guarding your mother.'

'Hey there, Maisie,' Masson called as they stopped at the gate. 'What's going on along the street? I heard shooting.'

'Your friend, Sol Kennedy, was shot dead,' Maisie replied with a touch of relief in her tone.

'Who killed him?' Masson demanded.

'I did.' Chet dropped his hand to his gun butt as Masson turned quickly to lunge into the house. 'Hold it right there,' he shouted as his gun came to hand.

Masson halted and turned, gun in his hand, but when he saw that Chat was covering him he released his weapon and raised his hands.

'What do you want?' he demanded. 'I ain't done anything against the law.'

'You're holding a woman here against her will,' Chet replied. 'Take me to her.'

'Did you tell him about this, Maisie?' Masson demanded. 'If you did you're in a whole heap of trouble now.'

'Get moving,' Chet said harshly. 'You've got more trouble on your shoulders than you can handle.'

Masson shrugged, went into the house with Chet almost on his heels, and led the way up the stairs. He unlocked a bedroom door. Chet thrust him inside and followed. His mother was seated on a bed, head in her hands.

'Are you OK, Ma?' Chet demanded, and she looked up when she recognized his voice.

Masson chose that moment to resist. He threw a punch at Chet's jaw, but Chet was watching him closely and took the blow on his shoulder. He swung his right arm and his pistol cracked against Masson's left temple. He dropped instantly. Chet glanced at Maisie, who had followed them into the house.

'Get my mother out of here,' he said. 'Take her to the hotel and stay with her until I show up.'

Chet helped his mother to her feet and Maisie took her arm. Mrs Hallam went eagerly. Chet bent over Masson, who was beginning to stir.

'On your feet,' he said. 'You're on your way to jail.

But first I want to know who you are and what you do around town.'

'I'm a friend of Sol Kennedy. We rode together.'

'That makes you an outlaw running with the Frazee gang,' Chet rapped. 'Kennedy was a gang member – him and Buck Allen. They came into town to take over the law. I've put a stop to that, and if Allen shows up around here again I'll arrest or kill him.'

Masson's face turned pale and he shook his head. 'That ain't so,' he protested. 'I've been a cowpoke all my working life.'

'Show me your hands.'

Masson shook his head and put his hands behind his back. Chet smiled.

'OK, you don't have to show me. You've already given me the answer. So start talking. Where is the gang holed up, and what are their plans?'

Masson did not reply.

'So what happened to my father when he disappeared?' Chet asked.

'Don't ask me. You need to talk to someone close to Frazee.'

'Are there any more of the gang in town, posing as honest men?'

'You're asking me questions about things I don't know.'

'So let's get over to the jail and I'll put you behind bars. A spell in there might help you get your memory back.'

'I'll do a deal with you.' Desperation appeared on

Masson's face. 'I'm small fry and don't amount to much. I'll trade some information if you forget about me, and I'll head on outa town and never come back.'

'What's the information?'

'It'll help you bust the set-up around here, and if you move fast you'll maybe grab Frazee and the gang.'

'Keep talking. If what you tell me adds up to a pile of beans then I'll see you get out of town.'

'Your brother, Arnie Mayhew, is in cahoots with Frazee. He's been passing information to the gang about shipments he carries on the stage.'

Chet felt a stab of mental pain as he digested the information.

'And that ain't all,' Masson continued, eagerness now edging his tone. 'Mayhew has his fingers in a couple more business pies around here. Ask him about the protection racket, and then hit him with the rustling.'

'I'll stick you behind bars until I've checked out what you've said. Head for the jail, and don't give me any more trouble.'

Masson started across the road with Chet behind him, and as they reached the opposite sidewalk two men crossed in front of the saloon, angling to reach Chet and his prisoner. Chet saw them, and their general appearance alerted him. Both were range-dressed, and they were well armed – pistols belted around their waists. They looked like long riders, gun hawks in a town where honest folk lived. One was tall and lean, dressed in black, his mean eyes moving ceaselessly as he checked his surroundings. The other was shorter, fair-haired; his lips thin, set in a permanent, mirthless grin. Chet stiffened for trouble.

As the pair drew closer, the shorter man dropped his hand to the gun holstered on his hip and called: 'Hey, Masson, are you in trouble with the law?'

'You could say that,' Masson replied instantly. 'Will you do something about it?'

The tall newcomer reached for his holstered gun in the fastest draw Chet had ever seen, and Chet, mentally geared for trouble, grasped his gun butt and drew the weapon, cocking it before it was lev-elled. He could see the shorter man pulling his gun, and the thought exploded in his brain that he was going to lose this one. He fired at the faster man before he was on line. The crash of the shot threw echoes across the street, and reverberated. Chet restrained his breathing as he worked his gun. The tall man fired as Chet triggered his first shot, which struck the tall man high in the right shoulder instead of finding the chest. The man's slug crackled in Chet's left ear as he twisted away, his tall figure folding at the waist. When he hit the ground he pushed his long face into the dust like a hog search-ing for food. But he rolled on to his back and lifted his gun for a second shot.

Chet shifted his aim to the shorter man, who was moving to his left because Masson, trying to get out of the line of fire, took the wrong direction and

107

placed himself between Chet and the gun. Chet dived to the ground, hit the dirt on his left shoulder, and triggered a shot as his weapon drew a bead. The gunman jerked at the impact of the .45 slug, which tore a hole in his belly, and he went down in a heap, losing his gun in the process and howling like a hound dog as pain speared through him. Chet swung his gun to cover the other man, and saw that he was now lying motionless on his face.

Masson, down on his hands and knees, jumped up and turned to run away. Chet pushed himself to one knee, covering Masson with the .45.

'Hold it, Masson, or I'll kill you,' Chet called.

Masson looked over his shoulder, stared into Chet's gun muzzle, and shifted his gaze to the two men down in the dust. He halted and raised his hands. Gun echoes faded slowly and men were appearing on the boardwalks, attracted by the sounds of more gun play. Chet got up and approached the smaller gunman. He kicked aside the discarded weapon, and a cursory glance at the man's wound convinced Chet that there would no further trouble from him.

He approached the second man, saw that he was bleeding heavily, and looked around quickly. The first of the townsmen was coming at a run across the street, and Chet shouted at him.

'Get the doctor here but fast. This man is bleeding to death.'

The townsman changed direction abruptly and ran off along the street. Chet called Masson, and the man approached, hands above his head.

'If you know anything about wounds then do something for him,' Chet said sharply, 'or he'll die before the doc gets here.'

Masson dropped to his knees beside the wounded man. He bared the wound in the chest. It was lower than Chet had figured, and blood was issuing from it. Masson stuck a thumb into the wound and the blood flow eased. He met Chet's hard gaze.

'I can hold him like this until the doc arrives,' Masson said.

'Who is he?' Chet demanded.

'I don't know. He's a stranger to me.'

'He called you by name, and he wouldn't have pulled his gun if he hadn't known you. Start telling me the truth, Masson, or you'll be behind bars for five years.'

'He's Joe McCall, one of the fastest gunnies in Kansas.'

'And what's the name of the other one?'

'Frank Clements. They ride with Frazee.'

'Outlaws, huh? That figures. Why were you guarding my mother in Kennedy's house? Kennedy also rode with Frazee. So why was he acting as a deputy here in town?'

'Frazee reckoned it would be easier for the gang if he controlled the local law.'

'Is that why my father disappeared?'

'Sure it was. He couldn't be bought or scared. He was lured out of town and rode into an ambush set up for him.'

'And they killed him?' Chet demanded.

'No, they didn't. He fought his way clear of the trap and disappeared. They never set eyes on him again. He was bad hit in the gun trap, and I reckon he fell off his horse and died out there on the prairie.'

'So why was Kennedy holding my mother in his house?'

'Frazee wanted to talk to her. They was gonna take her out to the hideout. Frazee reckons if your father is still alive then she knows where he is.'

'So where is the gang hiding out now?'

Masson shook his head. 'I reckon I've told you enough to escape being jailed. I don't know where the gang is right now. I heard they were planning a move, and they could be anywhere.'

There was movement on the street, and Chet looked round to see Doc Fletcher coming, followed by a small crowd of townsmen. The doctor arrived and paused to look down at McCall.

'You're doing a good job,' he observed. 'Can you hold him a few moments longer?'

'As long as it takes,' Masson said.

The doctor moved to Clements and dropped to one knee. After a cursory examination he straightened and looked at Chet.

'He's cashed his chips,' he remarked. 'I'll stop the bleeding on this one and take him along to my office. Is he under arrest?'

'That's for sure,' Chet told him. 'He rode with Frazee, the outlaw.'

'It's about time something was done about those hellions.' Fletcher set to work, applying his skill to stop the bleeding from McCall's wound. Chet stood watching, and when he was certain that the wounded man was not going to die summarily he motioned for Masson to get moving.

'I'll check with you later, Doc,' he said. 'I've got things to do that can't wait.'

'I've got some urgent work to do on this wound,' Fletcher said. He looked around at the crowd, called four names, and said. 'You four pick up this man and carry him carefully to my office.'

Chet waited until the wounded man was being removed from the street. Masson was growing impatient.

'I could sneak out of town real good right now,' he hinted.

'I'll have to check out your information before I can accept it,' Chet replied. 'Let's go.'

Masson shrugged and headed for the law department. Pete Sayer opened the office door, and grinned when he recognized Masson.

'What have you got him for?' he demanded.

'Hold him while I check out some facts,' Chet told him.

Sayer took Masson into the cell block and slammed a door on him. He came back into the office, grinning.

'You need to make a plan,' he said to Chet. 'When Frazee hears what you're doing around here he'll bring his bunch in and trample you in the dust.

You'd better get some armed men around you for back-up.'

'That sounds like good advice. Do you know any honest men around here who would act as a posse?'

'I'll talk to some dependable men and let you know what I come up with.'

'I've got a couple of things to handle. I'll come back here when I've checked them out.'

Chet left the department, and went quickly to the hotel, where he had told Maisie to wait with his mother. He found Ellen Whiteside in the foyer, looking anxious, and crossed to the desk to talk to her.

'I'm glad you're here,' she said quickly. 'Your mother is in the dining room with the saloon girl, Maisie. The saloon man, Wainwright, came in to see Maisie, and there was some shouting between them.'

'Thanks.' Chet walked into the dining room. His mother was seated at a table by the front window with Maisie beside her, both staring out of the window at the street. The big, well-dressed man Chet had seen outside the saloon when he and Maisie were on their way to Kennedy's house was leaning against a wall near Maisie.

'You'll do as you're told, Maisie,' Wainwright was saying. 'You ain't quitting. Nobody quits on me. You'll come back to the saloon now.'

He heard Chet entering the room and fell silent. His face was suffused with anger. He was tough-looking, wore a holstered gun on his right hip, and stared at Chet as if he was looking at his worst enemy.

'What's going on here?' Chet demanded.

'That ain't any business of yours,' said Wainwright sharply. 'Maisie works for me.'

Chet crossed the room and halted in front of Wainwright. 'She's leaving town on the next stage,' he said brusquely.

'The hell she is! She's not going anywhere.'

'Mister,' Chet said, 'when I give an order in the course of my law dealing then what I say goes. Maisie is leaving.'

'You can't order her around like that.'

'Try and stop me!' Chet gazed into Wainwright's flushed face. He saw intention in Wainwright's eyes and steeled himself for action.

Wainwright lifted his hands and smacked his right fist into the open palm of his left hand. The crack of flesh striking flesh echoed through the tall room. Chet moved instantly, his left fist flashing out in a powerful hook, his left foot sliding forward to transfer weight into the blow. His hard knuckles landed flush on Wainwright's jaw. The big man staggered under the impact and his legs began to buckle. His hands clenched into fists, but before he could get set, Chet caught him with a right-hand punch that struck him on the temple. Wainwright spun away and fell on his face, to lie unmoving.

'Gee!' Maisie gasped. 'I've seen him in a lot of fights, but I never saw him knocked off his feet before.' She went to Wainwright's side and gazed down at him, her eyes expressionless. Then she looked up at Chet. 'I won't feel safe with him walking around town,' she said. 'If I leave on the stage he'll send a man to take me off it and bring me right back here.'

'He won't be free to walk around town,' Chet said. 'I'll jail him until you get clear. Don't go back to the saloon. Stay here until I come for you. I'll escort you to the coach and send a man along to see you over the first ten miles. While you're here you can keep an eye on my mother. Will you do that?'

'Sure thing! But I need my clothes from the saloon.'

'I'll go with you later to collect what you need,' he responded. He saw Wainwright stirring and drew his pistol. 'Come on, Wainwright,' he rasped. 'You're gonna spend a couple of days in jail. On your feet and head out across the street.'

'Come and talk to me before you do anything else, Chet,' Mrs Hallam said, and Chet turned to face her. She looked as if she might collapse at any moment, but determination was prominent in her expression. 'This business is getting out of hand.' Her voice faltered. 'Only you can stop what's going on.'

'I'm doing what I can, and without help from anyone,' he responded. 'I'll come back to you, Ma. Stay here at the hotel and keep an eye on Maisie – you two can keep an eye on each other. I just don't know who I can trust around here.'

He ushered Wainwright out of the hotel and they crossed the street to the law office. He saw the saloon man safely into a cell and then returned to the street. He had to face his stepbrother, and he wasn't looking forward to the situation. Arnie, it seemed, had lined himself up with the bad men.

There were little knots of townsmen standing on the boardwalks, discussing the latest shooting, and Chet looked around for Arnie but did not see him. He went to the doctor's house, but Fletcher was not at home. Mrs Fletcher, a tall, thin woman with a kindly face, admitted him, and shook hands when he introduced himself.

'I'm glad you've found the time to call,' she said. 'Charley Barrett has been asking for you all morning. He won't settle at all. He's got something on his mind.' She paused as a thought struck her, and asked, 'You are here to see him, aren't you?'

'I'll see him now I'm here, but I'm looking for my brother, Arnie Mayhew. I was told he came to see Doc this morning.'

'He was here earlier. Doc checked him over and gave him permission to go back to work. Arnie said he had to take a coach out.'

'I'll catch up with him shortly. Now where is Barrett?'

Mrs Fletcher led him up the stairs and showed him into a back bedroom. Charlie Barrett was propped up on his back in a bed by the window. Mrs Fletcher withdrew, and Chet went to the bedside. Barrett looked up at him. He had a fever – his forehead was beaded with perspiration and his eyes were filled with the remoteness of shock.

'You asked to see me,' Chet said.

'I want to say I got it wrong about you,' Barrett replied. 'I shouldn't have pulled a gun on you.' He closed his eyes; groaned. 'I shouldn't have pulled my

115

gun on you at the livery barn. I was half-crazy with grief over the death of my son. I reckoned the law was responsible for what happened to my boy.'

'I didn't become a deputy until this morning,' Chet explained. 'And by that time your son was dead.'

'I know that now. I'm sorry for jumping the gun.' Barrett jerked convulsively, groaned and his head slipped off the pillow. He began breathing heavily through his gaping mouth.

Chet waited a few moments, but Barrett did not stir. He breathing seemed to get worse. The bullet wound in his right shoulder was heavily bandaged. Chet shook his head and turned away, intending to report to Mrs Fletcher. He opened the bedroom door, and heard a bedspring twang as Barrett's weight shifted suddenly. He swung around instantly; saw Barrett half-sitting up in bed, his senses miraculously restored. Barrett was holding a .41 pocket gun in his left hand, but was having difficulty levelling the weapon at Chet. His left arm was wavering and the muzzle of the deadly little gun swung in a hesitant circle.

For a heart-stopping moment Chet was transfixed, aware that he had walked into a gun set-up. But his reflexes were unimpaired and his brain reacted to the situation. He dropped to his left knee as he drew his pistol, and the weapon exploded in smoke and muzzle flame as it lifted to cover Barrett. The crash of the shot hammered through the house. Barrett was thrown backward by the impact of the slug, and dropped his gun on the bed as he died. . . .

EIGHT

Chet got to his feet and gazed at Barrett, unable to believe the rancher had tricked him. And Barrett was dead. Chet's slug had taken him through the heart – there had been no time for a wounding shot. The gun echoes were fading from the house, and Mrs Fletcher's feet thudded on the stairs as she returned to investigate the disturbance. She came into the room and paused, horror showing in her eyes as she regarded Barrett's body. She turned to Chet, who shook his head slowly.

'Don't ask me what happened,' he said. 'He was friendly until I turned my back, and then he pulled a gun. He had me cold but he wasn't fast enough. I'm wondering what he wanted besides aiming to kill me.'

He departed, shaken by his experience, and returned to the hotel. Ellen Whiteside was at the reception desk. She studied Chet's features before speaking, her own face exhibiting worry.

'I heard a shot a short time ago,' she said. 'Were

you involved?'

He nodded, but did not answer the question. 'Where's my mother?' he asked.

'She went to the saloon with Maisie, who is worried about getting her clothes. She thought that with Wainwright in jail she wouldn't have any trouble getting what she wants.'

Chet turned and hurried out of the hotel. He looked around the street. It looked quiet, but two men were walking along the boardwalk on the opposite side, and he dropped his hand to his gun butt when he recognized one as Buck Allen. The sheriff spotted him at the same time, left his companion instantly, and started across the street. Chet changed direction and went to meet the renegade.

'How are you doing?' Allen called as he closed the distance between them.

'Much better now I can see you,' Chet replied. 'I've been cleaning up. I killed Kennedy, and now you're here I can deal with you.'

Allen halted abruptly, his face changing expression. He dropped his right hand to the butt of his gun.

'Hold it,' Chet warned. 'You don't have to draw against me. Just raise your hands and I'll arrest you. I know you're one of Frazee's gang, and that you and Kennedy came here to take over the law. Tell me what happened to my father.'

The confrontation put Allen on the wrong foot. He gazed at Chet, who waited patiently, gun hand down at his side, the inside of his wrist touching the

118

butt of his pistol. Chet could almost see Allen's brain working, checking his chances, and the renegade must have come up with a solution to his problem because he set his right hand into action and clawed his pistol out of its holster.

Chet moved into his well-practised draw. His gun came out of leather and lifted in a single fluid movement, thumbing back the hammer before the weapon levelled. Allen was fast, but Chet was swifter. He triggered his gun as it lined up on the sheriff's chest. The crash of the shot threw echoes around the street. Allen reared backwards, dropping his gun before it could cover Chet. He followed it down into the dust with blood showing around the hole that had suddenly appeared on his chest front.

The man across the street who had been walking with Allen stopped dead in his tracks when he heard the shot, and Chet, looking towards him, saw him pull his gun. Chet lifted his pistol and sent a shot over the man's head. The man threw down his gun and raised his hands shoulder high. Chet went over to him. The man was tall and heavily-built, dressed in range clothes, and he had the look of a long rider about him. His face was more than half covered with a bushy black beard. His dark eyes looked mean, and had a hunted expression in them that Chet knew only too well.

'What's your name?' Chet demanded.

'Slick McCord.'

'You were with Buck Allen. How'd you know him?'

'I don't know him. I met him out of town. We were

119

both coming in this direction and rode in together.'

'I don't believe you.' Chet spoke harshly. 'I've got you figured as an outlaw – one of Frazee's gang – and I'm gonna put you behind bars until I've had a chance to check you out. Head along the street; I'll direct you to the jail.' He motioned with his gun.

McCord shrugged and went forward. Chet followed him. Pete Sayer, waiting at the iron door sealing off the law office and cells, was holding a shotgun.

'What was the shooting about?' he demanded when Chet arrived with his prisoner.

'I just killed Buck Allen,' Chet replied. 'He didn't fancy seeing the inside of your jail, Pete. This man is Slick McCord. I suspect him of being an outlaw. Check him out when you've locked him up.'

'He looks familiar to me,' Sayer said. 'I reckon we've got a dodger on him.'

Chet ran his hands over McCord, and sat down at the desk while Sayer took the prisoner through to the cells. Sayer returned after a few moments, and lifted a stack of wanted notices out of a desk drawer. He gave half to Chet and sat down at a corner of the desk with the other half. They were silent for some moments while they looked at the faces on the dodgers, and then Chet found himself gazing at a likeness of Slick McCord.

'Here he is,' Chet said. 'Jay McCord wanted for robbery. There's a reward of $500 for his arrest. It says here he is a member of Mitch Frazee's gang.'

Sayer grinned. 'It'll be the day when you haul in

Frazee,' he said. 'I reckon you can do it, if anyone can.'

'Bring McCord back out here,' Chet said. 'I wanta find out if he knows anything about my father.'

Sayer went back into the cells, and returned with McCord, who sat down on the chair in front of the desk. Sayer stood behind him, a pistol in his hand. McCord was sullen now. He stared at a spot on the desk and refused to meet Chet's eyes.

'It didn't take me long to get the lowdown on you,' said Chet, and pushed the wanted notice across the desk.

McCord looked at the dodger and then averted his eyes.

'Where's Frazee hiding out on the range?' Chet demanded.

McCord shook his head. 'You don't expect me to tell you, huh? I ain't gonna say a word.'

'What happened to Sheriff Hallam?'

'That tough old guy! He was brought to the hideout about a month ago. A couple of the boys took him out. I never saw him again.'

A pang stabbed through Chet's breath at the words. His expression did not change but a wave of anger spread through him. He clenched his teeth and drew a deep breath. When he spoke his voice was steady but low pitched.

'He was my father, and I want the men who killed him. Put names to them, McCord.'

'That's more than my life is worth. If I did, and the word got around, I'd be hunted down and killed.'

Chet realized that he would get nothing from

121

McCord, and signed to Sayer to take the man back to his cell. He sat looking at the dodgers, and came across one that depicted the face of Mitch Frazee, who was wanted for murder and robbery, with a price of $2,000 on his head. Frazee was big and fleshy, his blunt features looking as if they had been stuck on his round face as an afterthought. The travails of his past were stamped into his expression. His eyes carried a blend of viciousness and defiance – a man without mercy or compassion.

'What are you gonna do now?' Sayer asked when he came back into the office.

'I've got a couple of things to look into, but I really need to get out on the range with a posse and hunt down Frazee and his crooked bunch.'

Chet got to his feet and Sayer let him out of the office. He went along the street to the saloon and shouldered through the batwings, fearing that Maisie might change her mind about leaving.

Mrs Hallam was inside, seated at a small table. There were roughly a dozen men in the saloon. Some were at the bar and others were seated at the tables. Chet went to his mother and sat down opposite her. She looked intently at him, and then sighed.

'I told you to stay in the hotel,' Chet said.

'Maisie wanted me to come here with her. She won't be long, and then we'll go back to the hotel.'

'You'd make life a lot easier for me if you'd do as I tell you,' he retorted. He looked around the saloon when a commotion sounded at the far end and saw Maisie descending the flight of stairs that gave access to the upper storey. She was carrying a couple of cases, and the bar tender was behind her, remonstrating loudly.

'I got orders to keep you here until Wainwright gets out of jail, Maisie.'

'You better talk to that new deputy,' Maisie replied. 'He told me to get out of town on the next stage, and that's what I'm gonna do.'

Chet got to his feet as Maisie came towards him. She grinned when she saw him waiting, and dropped her cases at his feet. The 'tender came to her side and halted. He gazed intently at Chet, his eyes filled with hostility. Chet felt a pang of impatience strike through his breast.

'What's your problem?' he demanded. 'I heard Maisie tell you she was leaving town on my say-so.'

'You're the law.' The barkeep shrugged. 'There's nothing I can do about that.'

'Just keep that in mind,' Chet told him. 'Come on, Maisie. Back to the hotel until it's time for the coach to leave.'

'Wainwright ain't gonna like this,' the 'tender said.

'Come with me, if you're so minded. I'll lock you in the same cell with him and you can tell him all about it.'

The man shook his head and went behind the bar.

Chet picked up one of Maisie's cases and she lifted the other. Mrs Hallam got to her feet and walked to the batwings. Maisie followed her and Chet brought up the rear, his right hand close to the butt of his holstered gun. He was tensed for trouble but nothing

123

happened, and he sighed with relief when they were on the street.

'After this you'll both do exactly what I tell you,' he said as they walked into the hotel. 'I've got another matter to attend to before I can get down to my main chore, and I don't need to be side-tracked. So stay put in here until I get back to you.'

'When are you going out after the gang?' asked Mrs Hallam.

'I'm near enough ready to turn my attention to Frazee and his bunch, and after that I shall be free to look for Pa.'

'He's dead,' Mrs Hallam said in a low tone.

'You don't know that for certain,' Chet said. 'Don't give up hope yet. You'd better go up to your room, Ma, and take Maisie with you. And do as you're told after this, Maisie. Stay with my mother and keep out of sight. I'll be back shortly, and then we'll take a fresh look at the situation.'

He ushered them up to his mother's room, and sighed with relief when he closed the door on them. He left the hotel and went in search of Arnie, and his impatience fled as he cleared his mind and prepared for the confrontation. He had some hard questions for his half-brother to answer.

But he drew a blank when he called at the Lomax house. Annie Lomax answered the door, and was looking worried.

'Arnie isn't back from the doctor's yet,' she told Chet. 'I was about to go looking for him.'

'He saw the doctor earlier,' Chet told her, 'but left

124

soon after. Have you any idea where he might be?'

'With my father, I hope,' Annie replied.

'You stay here. I'll take a look,' he said. 'I need to talk to him.'

'Is he in trouble with you?' she asked hesitantly.

He looked into her eyes, saw worry lurking in their depths, and felt a pang of sympathy for her.

'Do you expect him to be in trouble?' he countered in a softer tone, holding her gaze.

'No-o! He works very hard for my father. But from what he's said about you, it seems that you make trouble for him whenever you can.'

'I know he thinks that, but I can assure you I've never done anything against him. Any trouble between us has always come from him. I need to talk to him and straighten out some problems, but I need to find out if my father is still alive, and if so, where he is right now.'

She nodded, still gripped by worry, and Chet left her and departed to walk to the office on Main Street. He found Matt Lomax there, but no sign of Arnie.

'I haven't seen Arnie yet this morning,' Lomax said when he learned of Chet's business. 'I know he was going to see the doctor. He wants to get back to work as soon as possible. I don't think he's ready yet, but then he's like that. He can never do enough. Say, you're making quite a stir in town. I've been hearing shots all morning, and there's always someone calling in to pass on the news. You're certainly cleaning up, and no mistake. But Frazee and his gang are the ones you really need to tackle.'

'I've been held up by minor problems,' Chet replied, 'but I'm getting to the point where I'll be able to concentrate on Frazee. That's why I wanta talk to Arnie. He's the only one in town who has been in contact with the gang.'

'He had to duck lead every time he met them,' Lomax said.

'When you see him, tell him I need to talk to him. I'll be at the hotel for a bit. He can find me there.'

'I'll pass the word,' Lomax said.

Chet left the office. His mind was clearing. Since his arrival in town he had been beset by law business, which had to be cleared before he could concentrate on learning what had happened to his father. He had no idea if his father was dead or alive, but his wish that the old man had survived Frazee's death sentence kept him brimming with hope. He glanced around the street, missing nothing and, when he saw Maisie emerge from the hotel to hurry along the sidewalk to her left, he followed her eagerly.

Maisie was alert to her surroundings. Twice she glanced around the street, and Chet stepped into an alley and then a shop doorway to avoid being seen. Maisie moved as if she had a definite direction in mind, and he stayed behind her. It was in his mind that Arnie had arranged for Maisie to come to this town when she left Texas.

When Maisie reached the door of a small bar she paused and checked the street again. Chet moved into a doorway. When he peered out, Maisie was no longer in sight, and the door of the bar was closing. He hurried forward and entered the bar. The place was empty except for a big man in a white apron polishing glasses behind the bar.

'Where's Maisie?' Chet demanded, crossing to the bar.

'Who's Maisie?' the man replied. He was over six feet tall, powerfully built, with heavy shoulders and ham-like fists. His head looked too small for his body; his features showed the bruising effects of years of fighting with his fists. He gazed at Chet with hostility in his dark eyes, and his left hand strayed under the bar.

'She came in here just ahead of me; I was almost on her heels so I know she's here, so where has she gone?'

'That ain't any of your business. You can't come in here throwing your weight around. I've heard about you – the old sheriff's son. Your father was a nosey man, and it looks like you take after him.'

'The woman I followed in here has been ordered to leave town on the next stage, and I'm the one that has to see she obeys the order. So tell me where she is.'

'And if I don't?'

Chet drew his gun with a single flick of his right wrist, and the gaping muzzle pointed at the big man's chest. He cocked the gun, the three clicks sounding heavy with menace.

'I've asked you the question more than once, mister, and usually I don't repeat myself. So you're on borrowed time now, and you better think carefully before you open your mouth again. Where is Maisie?'

The man stared into the steady muzzle covering him. His mouth opened slightly, but he thought better of speaking. He moistened his thick lips, withdrew his left hand from under the bar, and his fingers were clasped around a pistol. As he cocked it, Chet struck with his gun, slamming the long barrel against the man's gun hand. The weapon fell from his grasp and thudded on the bar. The man tried to scoop it up with his right hand, but Chet was moving forward, his gun swinging, and he struck again with the weapon, crashing the barrel against the side of the big man's head.

The bar shook when the 'tender hit the floor. He tried to rise but could not make it, and fell inertly as his senses fled. Chet looked around. There was a door in the back wall, situated in the space where the bar ended. He went to it, eased it open, and walked into a store room containing stacks of crates of beer. Maisie was standing at the far end of the room, partly concealed by crates, and talking to someone out of Chet's sight.

'I had to come and see you, Arnie,' Maisie was saying in a high-pitched tone. 'You must know what's happening. Chet is throwing his weight around. I've got to be on the next stage out of town, and he's on my neck all the time.'

'Where's the dough?' Arnie demanded, and Chet, shocked by his brother's presence, stepped into cover behind a pile of beer crates. 'Are you trying to run a sandy on me, Maisie? You want all the dough for yourself, huh? But don't try that one on me because it won't wash. Forget about my brother. You ain't leaving town. And stay close to that money. I put in a lot of work to get it. When you leave town you will be with me, and the dough goes with us. Now get out of here before you're spotted, and stick close to the dough. Where have you got it hidden?'

'In the case you put the false bottom in. It's safe enough. But you'll have to do something about Chet.'

'He'll be taken care of when the time comes. I'm waiting to see Frazee shortly. We're gonna clean out the bank and then hit the trail. I'll be driving the coach you'll be leaving on, so what have you got to worry about?'

'I don't believe you intend to leave the set-up you've got here,' Maisie said. 'You're gonna marry the boss's daughter and take over the freighting business.'

'I was gonna do that.' Arnie laughed harshly. 'And then Chet turned up, and all that business has gone out of the window. So I'm gonna get out while the going is good, and we'll have enough dough to make a fresh start where neither of us are known. Just do like I say and everything will work out OK.'

'I'll go back to the hotel,' Maisie said reluctantly. 'I've got no choice. I have to trust you.'

Chet turned and went back into the bar, not wishing to confront Arnie at this time. The big bartender lay motionless on the floor, and Chet hurried to the door before Maisie appeared. As he stepped out to the sidewalk he almost collided with a man in the act of entering the bar. They both pulled to a halt, a foot apart. Chet looked into the newcomer's face and a thrill stabbed through him when he recognized the harsh features of Mitch Frazee, the outlaw gang boss. . . .

NINE

Chet saw Frazee glance at the law badge on his chest, and the sight of it set the outlaw into frenzied action. He cursed as he grabbed the butt of his gun. His elbow bent, and the big pistol on his hip seemed to leap out of leather. Chet did not want to shoot, because the gunshot would warn Arnie of trouble. He reached out with his left hand, grasped Frazee's gun wrist, and forced it aside as he threw a punch with his right hand. His knuckles crashed against Frazee's jaw. The outlaw sagged, but retained his grasp on the gun.

Chet lifted his knee to Frazee's groin and slammed it home. Frazee hunched over with a cry of pain. Chet lifted his knee again, striking Frazee in the face. The outlaw fell backwards. His hand slid from his gun, and Chet snatched it and turned it to cover the outlaw.

Maisie emerged from the bar and paused, gasping in shock. Chet glanced at her. She moved away from him and leaned against a wall for support.

'Get out of here,' Chet told her roughly. 'Go back to the hotel and stay there like I told you.' He returned his attention to the prostrate Frazee.

'Do you know who he is?' Maisie demanded, staring at Frazee.

'Yeah, he's Mitch Frazee. Now get out of here.'

'I hope you know what you're doing,' she gasped, and hurried away towards the hotel.

Chet nudged Frazee with the toe of his boot. 'Come on, get on your feet. I didn't think it would be this easy to take you. You must have been half asleep.'

Frazee writhed in pain, and when he tried to get up he fell sideways and remained down. At that moment, Chet felt the muzzle of a six-gun press against the back of his neck, and Arnie's voice hissed in his ear.

'Drop your gun,' Arnie said. 'Mitch, can you get up?'

Frazee staggered to his feet as Chet's gun hit the sidewalk. He snatched up the weapon and covered Chet. There was deadly intention in his face, and Arnie spoke sharply.

'No rough stuff, Mitch. You've got some important business to take care of. Get the hell out of here and I'll see you later, like we arranged.'

Frazee threw down Chet's gun and turned away to the nearest alley. Arnie removed his gun muzzle from Chet's neck.

'Pick up your gun and come with me,' Arnie said sharply.

Chet was relieved by the feel of his gun in his hand.

132

'What about Frazee?' he demanded. 'I want him and his gang.'

'We'll do it my way. Let's get our horses.'

'What are you up to?' Chet asked.

'Now is not the time for questions. If you want Frazee and his bunch then come with me.'

Chet did not trust Arnie, but the chance of taking the outlaws was too good to be missed. Arnie had holstered his gun and was moving away from the bar. Chet slid his Colt back into its holster and hurried after him. Arnie went along the sidewalk to the livery barn. Chet decided he had nothing to lose by waiting to discover what was on his brother's mind. He saddled his horse, and joined Arnie at the rear door where he was waiting with his horse. The animal had been ready-saddled, Chet noticed.

'Where are we going?' Chet demanded. 'Frazee is in town. This is not the way to catch him.'

'You always did ask too many questions,' Arnie replied. 'For once in your life just do like I say.'

Chet shrugged and followed Arnie out the back door of the barn. They circled around a corral, and Arnie put his mount into a lope out of town. Chet matched him stride for stride and they rode to the north trail and followed it. Chet was mystified, and curious. He stayed with Arnie, who set a fast pace along the trail. When his curiosity became too great, Chet tried to draw Arnie out, but received a shake of the head.

As time passed, Chet began to feel that he was making a mistake. He knew from experience that he could not trust Arnie, and the men he wanted were probably all in town. Was Arnie leading him away to give Frazee a free hand for some illegal business? But despite his misgiving, he continued to ride at his brother's side. Questions burning in Chet's mind were almost too hot to consider. Despite the talk around town about Arnie's fight against the gang, Arnie had been on good terms with the gang boss – had ordered him away when Frazee was about to shoot Chet, and Frazee had gone without protest. Then there was the part-conversation Chet had over-heard between Arnie and Maisie – they were planning to leave town together, and Maisie was carrying cash – obviously stolen – in a case Arnie had fitted with a false bottom.

Chet dragged his mind from his thoughts and kept a watchful eye on his surroundings. He could not trust Arnie. The knowledge was uppermost in his mind, and it bothered him.

They travelled some ten miles before a ranch house appeared in the distance. Arnie glanced at Chet, and gave him a lop-sided grin.

'This is where the gang has been hiding out for the last week,' Arnie said. 'Frazee's in town robbing the bank with four of his gang backing him.'

'You got me out of the way so the bank could be robbed!' Chet rapped. He started to pull his horse around to ride back to town, but Arnie reached out and grasped his rein.

'Hold hard!' he rapped. 'You'll not get back to town in time to stop the robbery, and right now

Frazee is heading back here with the dough. What we have to do is get the drop on the rest of the gang here, and then set a gun trap for Frazee when he rides in.'

'You've planned this down to the last detail, huh?' Chet demanded. 'And what happens to me when the gang is finished? I don't think you'll hand the stolen dough back to the bank. I overheard you and Maisie talking back there in that bar. You're planning to run out with the money.'

'You'll get all the credit for smashing Frazee's gang.' Arnie chuckled harshly. 'What more do you want?'

'What happened to my father?'

Arnie's expression hardened. 'Why ask me? Him and me, we never did see eye to eye about anything. I don't know if he's dead or alive. It's your job to find out.'

Chet looked at the ranch house. 'How do you figure to take these men?' he asked.

'I can get them with no trouble. They know me well enough. But you're on their list to be killed. I reckon I could get away with taking you in at gun-point, and getting the drop on them while they're wondering about you. I can't fight them all. There'll be around six of them. Put your gun in your waist-band and, when I start shooting, you join in and we'll wipe them out.'

'And you'll save a slug for me when you've finished them, huh?' Chet laughed harshly. 'That sounds like a typical deal from you. OK, so take me in there as a prisoner. I'll go along with it. But be careful not to point your gun my way or you'll be dodging my slugs.'

Chet drew his pistol and stuck it in the waistband of his pants on his left hip. His jacket covered the butt. They continued to the ranch, and Arnie circled to the left as they drew nearer, aiming to enter the house by the back door, but a voice called to them from the front porch, and Chet saw a man standing in the doorway, a rifle in his hands.

'What the hell are you doing, sneaking in like that?' The man raised the muzzle of the rifle suggestively, but grinned. 'You're testing us to see if we're on our toes, huh?'

'I ain't sneaking around,' Arnie replied. 'I'm here to tell you Frazee walked into the bank as we left town. He should have the dough by now, and I'm gonna wait here to get my share of it.'

'Come on in then. Who's that with you, and why is he wearing a deputy badge?'

'Buck Allen and Kennedy are wearing law badges, ain't they? And this is my brother Chet Hallam.'

They entered the house. Four hard-eyed outlaws were sitting at a table, playing poker. Stacks of greenbacks and bottles of whiskey were on the table. Cigarette smoke was thick. The men were playing raucously. They did not look up as Arnie entered the room. Arnie moved away from Chet and approached the table as if interested in the game. Chet saw him reach for his gun. Chet turned to face the man who had been standing in the doorway, who had tucked the butt of the rifle into his right armpit, and was alert-eyed.

Arnie drew and cocked his gun and began shooting without warning. Chet drew his pistol when Arnie's first shot smacked into the nearest card player. The man with the rifle stepped backward half a step and began to lift his long gun. Chet shot him in the chest and turned swiftly to cover the men at the table. Arnie was fanning his gun, sending a stream of lead at the outlaws. The house shook to the blast of gunfire. Smoke flared and thunderous echoes tore through the silence. Arnie's face was a mask of raw brutality. The card players didn't have a chance. Hot lead battered them in a slaughterhouse action, and they fell from their chairs, blood spurting. It was all over in seconds.

Chet stepped back and held his smoking gun pointing at the floor. Arnie shot all four of the card players, and then turned to look for the man Chet had shot. Arnie straightened and smiled.

'I reckoned you could handle one,' he said. 'Now all we've got to do is wait for Frazee to turn up with the bank dough.'

'There was no need to massacre these men,' Chet said harshly. 'We could have disarmed them. And I thought your arm was injured in a fight with the outlaws.'

'I lied about that.' Arnie grinned. 'Let's get on with this. Frazee will have at least four men with him when he comes, and I ain't taking any chances on losing that dough.'

137

Chet did not expect to have to dodge Arnie's slugs until after the rest of the gang had been dealt with. He reloaded the empty chamber in his pistol and holstered it, feeling uneasy with gun smoke pervading his nostrils and aggravating his stomach. He turned to the porch door.

'Don't leave the house,' Arnie warned quickly. 'The best thing you can do is go upstairs and watch from the bedrooms. Come down when you spot the outlaws riding in and we'll start shooting as they dismount at the porch. We'll need to get them in a cross fire.'

Chet mounted the stairs and opened the doors of three bedrooms. He walked around the rooms, checking them, and then entered the front room, which overlooked the yard. He stood at a window, watching the approaches. His ears were still protesting at the blast of shooting, and he yawned to get his hearing back to normal. He thought of his father as he waited out the minutes. He heard nothing from Arnie, and wondered what he was doing. He had evidently planned every move to get rid of the outlaws and secure the stolen money. Further treachery was building up, and Chet steeled himself to be ready for Arnie's first hostile move.

Despite his wandering thoughts, Chet maintained his alertness, and about an hour later he spotted a faint movement on the trail that came from town. He ran to the door of the room.

'Arnie,' he shouted down the stairs. 'There's movement out on the trail.'

138

'I'm watching it,' Arnie replied. 'Have you got a good field of fire? You could shoot down at them when they pull up in the yard. But hold your fire until I start shooting.'

Chet went back to the window, and drew his pistol when he saw a lone rider jogging into the yard on a grey horse. It took him a moment to identify the newcomer as a woman, and was shocked when he recognized Maisie, dressed in denim pants and a tunic-type brown shirt – her feet were pushed into calf-high riding boots. The Stetson she was wearing hid her hair, the wide brim shading her face. A large travelling case was tied behind the cantle.

Arnie stepped into view in the yard below, and Chet fancied that his brother had known that Maisie was coming here. Arnie grasped the grey's reins when the animal stopped in front of him, and Maisie almost fell out of the saddle into his ready arms. Chet eased open the bedroom window. He could hear their voices plainly when they spoke.

'So you got here!' Arnie commented. 'Did you see anything of Frazee after you left me in town?'

'I saw Chet holding him at gunpoint outside the bar, so I didn't waste any time. I went for my case and then picked up this horse at the stable.'

'I'd better get you and the horse out of sight until we've handled the gang.' Arnie put an arm around Maisie's shoulder and led her and the horse off to the left and around the back of the house.

Chet remained alert but his thoughts were deep and fast. Arnie was playing his cards close to his vest.

He was supposed to be taking out the next stage from town, but it was obvious now that he would pull out when he'd got some of the bank money from the outlaws. Chet thought of Annie Lomax, waiting worriedly in town for Arnie to get home while he was planning to flee without a word to anyone – walking out on her and throwing in his job with her father.

He spotted dust rising in the air in the direction of the trail to town; coming quickly towards the ranch. He checked his pistol, and kept it in his hand as he watched and waited. A few moments later five riders appeared, travelling fast. When they entered the yard, Chet cocked his gun. There was no sign of Arnie, and no sound from him. Chet moistened his dry lips and, as the riders halted in front of the porch, he recognized Frazee and called a warning – giving the outlaws a chance to surrender.

'Throw up your hands and don't move. This is the law. You're all covered.'

For a split second the five men remained motionless. Frazee was on the left, two bulging saddlebags tied behind his saddle. He looked up at the window where Chet was standing, and reached for his gun. The other four men reacted instinctively – pulled their weapons and prepared to fight. Frazee got off his first shot, and glass tinkled from the window beside Chet's head. He depressed his muzzle until the foresight was lined up on the outlaw's chest.

He fired quickly. Gun smoke flared, blurring his target. Frazee swayed to the right in his saddle, but recovered his balance and whirled his horse around to ride for the nearest cover. Chet turned his attention to the other outlaws. Four pistols turned their fire on the upper window. Chet threw himself sideways to the floor and then got to his feet and moved to a second window. He smashed out a pane of glass, and heard gunfire down below. He looked down at the yard and saw Frazee sitting low in his saddle, galloping back towards the gate. The four riders were splitting up, drawing apart and heading fast in different directions. Two of them twisted in their saddles and threw lead at the bedroom window.

Chet ignored them and concentrated on Frazee. The outlaw was unsteady in his saddle, but he approached the gate, spurring hard to get more speed from his horse. Chet lifted his pistol, but at that moment a shot hammered from the porch and a slug smashed another pane of glass close to him. He peered down and saw gun smoke flaring out from the porch. Arnie was in action. Chet turned his gun on the other outlaws. One of them was sliding out of his saddle, and then another bit the dust. Chet aimed for another, and when he fired, the rider vacated his saddle. The remaining rider was riding out through the gateway when Arnie fired again. The man fell backwards out of his saddle, one foot caught in a stirrup, and he was dragged out to the trail, where the horse slowed and then halted.

Chet reloaded his gun. He gazed across the yard, and saw Frazee in the distance, still in his saddle and riding into cover. The echoes of the shooting were already fading into the background. He heard Arnie on the porch, shouting furiously because Frazee had gotten away. Chet looked from the window, and saw Maisie running across the yard to the nearest fallen outlaw. She ignored the man and looked in the saddlebags, and then turned to the watching Arnie and shook her head. He shouted for her to check the others. Maisie finished her chore and came back to the porch shaking her head. Frazee had escaped with all of the stolen money.

'Come on down, Chet,' Arnie yelled. 'It's all over. I'm gonna ride out after Frazee.'

Chet started to the bedroom door, intending to go down the stairs, but something in Arnie's voice alerted him and he went through to a back bedroom, opened the window and peered out. There was a lean-to shed under the window. He slid over the windowsill and lowered himself on to the roof of the shed. Silence pressed in around him as he dropped to the ground. He went to his left to a rear corner of the house and ran to the front corner. When he peered around the corner at the porch he saw Maisie beside Arnie, who was facing the door of the house, his gun levelled at the doorway.

A mirthless grin tugged at Chet's lips. So this was the pay-off. Arnie was planning to kill him. He almost wished that he had gone down the stairs to confront Arnie face to face. He stepped cautiously on to the porch and took a slow step towards his brother.

'Come on, Chet, where are you?' Arnie shouted, his gun steady, covering the doorway. 'It's all over. Frazee is getting away and we need to get after him.'

142

'I'm here, Arnie.' Chet spoke through stiff lips. His gun was in his hand, pointing downwards but ready for action. He was unhappy with the situation. He did not want to face Arnie yet in a showdown.

Arnie jerked his hand around and fired without apparently aiming. Chet felt the smash of the slug as it hammered into his right forearm. His pistol flew from his hand as pain slashed through his arm. Arnie fired again but his hammer struck an empty cartridge. Chet dived for his pistol, having to use his left hand and, as his fingers closed around the butt, Arnie lunged towards him and struck him solidly on the left temple with the long barrel of his empty gun. Chet fell forward on his face as his senses fled. . . .

TEN

Cold water splashed over Chet's face. Shock cut through the blankness misting his senses and jerked him into awareness. He opened his eyes, gasping, and looked up into Maisie's anxious face. She was holding a big jug that dripped water. He looked around, and saw he was lying on the porch. There was no sign of Arnie. Maisie dropped to her knees at his side.

'Where's Arnie?' he demanded, squeezing his eyes tightly closed. He lifted his right hand to touch his head, and gasped in pain as he moved the limb, which fell back limply to his side.

'He's gone,' Maisie said. 'He rode out twenty minutes ago.'

Chet tried to get up, but pain in his right forearm pinned him down, and he sensed that Arnie's bullet had broken a bone. He groaned, and then cursed.

'You think you've got trouble?' Maisie cut in, her face harshly set. 'Arnie's left me flat; even took the money that was in the bottom of my case. Heck, some of that dough was mine, earned in the saloon! He was gonna shoot you, Chet, but I talked him out of it. And I'm sure I don't know why I bothered. I'm left stranded without a dime, facing jail, but I've done what I can for you – bandaged you and stopped the bleeding, knowing that when you can get on your feet you'll stick me behind bars.'

'Stop your tongue wagging, Maisie, and tell me about Arnie. He must have made plans with you. I need to jail him. Get my horse. It's out back. Which way did Arnie ride?' The questions flowed from him in a disjointed fashion.

'Don't be a fool, Chet. The only way you're gonna get out of here is if I get a wagon and haul you back to town. You need a doctor. Your right arm is in a bad way. Forget about Arnie for now.'

'So you can meet up with him someplace else, huh?' He used his left hand to push his body into a sitting position, and leaned his back against the front wall of the house. He looked at his arm. Blood was still oozing from the wound, and the pain was unbearable. He clenched his teeth and reached for his gun with his left hand, but could not reach it. 'Give me the gun,' he commanded. 'I feel naked without it. There might be some stray outlaws around.'

Maisie stared at him for several seconds, then shrugged her slim shoulders, reached for his gun, and handed it to him.

'Can you work a gun with your left hand?' she demanded.

145

'I'm only slightly slower with my left, but my accuracy is the same whichever hand I use. Get my horse; I need to be riding.'

'Are you gonna kill Arnie?'

'Not if I can help it. Now get moving. While you're gabbing here, he's getting away.'

'What about me?' she persisted.

'I don't have time to consider you. I want Arnie and Frazee, and if I take them alive I'll jail them. What you do is up to you. If you're not around when I ride into town I won't come looking for you. But you better go a far piece, and ensure that we never meet up again. You got that?'

'You're all heart, Chet.'

'So get my horse and I'll be riding.'

Maisie jumped up, and ran into the house and through to the back door. Chet levered himself to his feet and stood with his back against the wall. He unfastened a couple of buttons and eased his right hand inside his shirt. The pain lessened as he relaxed the limb. Maisie came around the corner of the house, riding her horse and leading Chet's animal. She swung out of the saddle and trailed his reins.

'You're in no fit state to go after Arnie and Frazee,' she said.

'I'm sure you're right, but that ain't gonna stop me.' He stepped off the porch and grasped his reins with his left hand, then paused. 'You got any money at all?' he asked.

'Not even a wooden nickel. Arnie cleaned me out. But don't worry about me. I'll get by.'

146

He reached into his right breast pocket and produced a billfold – extracted a $20 bill and held it out to her. She shook her head and put her hands behind her back as if to resist temptation.

'I can't take that,' she said sharply. 'I ain't done right by you, Chet, and it sticks in my craw.'

He tucked the bill in her top pocket, and slapped her hand away when she reached for it.

'You'd better not go back to town,' he said. 'You'll only get into more trouble. Head on out – west, I should think. Now get going.'

'You're not gonna manage with your right arm busted,' she observed. 'If we ride together, I can look out for you.'

'You think I need a woman to take care of me?' He laughed harshly. 'Go on and get out of here. This is the last chance you're getting to make a good life for yourself. Now beat it, Maisie, and good luck.'

'I made a mistake when I left Texas to come here,' she said, her tone quivering.

'That was after the mistake you made before you left. I gave you a last chance then and you didn't take it. Now you want another last chance.' He paused and looked into her eyes, saw contrition in their depths, and a sigh escaped him. 'You did save me from Arnie,' he mused. 'I guess I owe you something for that.' He nodded. 'Go on back to town, stick with my mother, and we'll talk some more when I get through out here.'

'Do you mean that, Chet?' Her blue eyes shone, and it was like the sun coming out on a rainy day.

'Gee! You won't be sorry. I'll stay on the straight and narrow trail after this.'

She swung into her saddle and rode off quickly as if afraid he would change his mind. She did not look at him as she crossed the yard at a walking pace. When she reached the gate she looked back and gazed at him. Chet did not move. He was unemotional, empty. Maisie heeled her horse and set off at a trot, and was riding at a lope by the time she disappeared from his sight.

Chet shook his head. He checked his gun and stuck it in his waistband. He grasped the saddle horn with his left hand, stuck his left toe in the stirrup, and swung into the saddle. Pain flared through the injured arm as he bumped his elbow against his thigh. He touched spurs to his mount and left the ranch, his teeth clenched against the pain assailing him; focused his mind on what he had to do.

He reined in outside the gate, reliving the moment when Frazee had fled, and his keen gaze studied the dust. He saw fresh prints heading away and set out to follow them. The sun was hot on his back and shoulders as he pushed for a mile-eating lope, and he was aware that a second set of hoof prints was on the trail before him – Arnie's.

The trail veered to the north and, a couple of hours later, it turned east. Chet sat slumped in his saddle, his arm tortured by the jolting movement, his gaze set on the prints he was following. This was unknown country to him, but the tracks were a link to the men he wanted, and he would not give up the trail. Retribution was at his shoulder. The guilty men had to be killed or brought to justice.

He stirred in the saddle when he spotted buzzards circling lazily in the sky ahead. He frowned, aware of what their presence meant – an animal or a man was down in the dust. He roused himself from his lethargy and looked around. The Kansas sky was high and wide. No living creature was to be seen on the illimitable prairie.

He went on, bothered by the glare of the sun. He saw a small herd of cattle in the distance, and guessed there was a ranch somewhere close. The tracks continued almost in a straight line to the spot over which the buzzards were circling, and when he topped a skyline he reined back quickly and sought cover as a bullet crackled past his head. He jarred his arm getting out of the saddle, but grasped his gun and dropped on to his left side; edged forward until he could peer over the crest.

A man was seated on the ground, holding a rifle in his hands, his right leg stuck out awkwardly in front of him. His horse was motionless on the ground a few yards from him. Chet's lips pulled into a thin line when he recognized Arnie, and he studied the ground to find the best way of approaching him without getting shot.

He eased off the crest and went to his horse, hauled himself into the saddle, and rode to the right to circle Arnie's position. He found a depression that headed in the direction he wanted, left his horse in cover, and moved in on Arnie from behind – the fallen horse between them. When he had a clear view of Arnie he cocked his pistol. Arnie heard the sound and swung round. When he saw Chet behind him with levelled gun he froze, his expression showing desperation.

'Get rid of your gun,' Chet rasped, 'or I'll kill you.'

'My horse put a foot into a gopher hole and broke its damn leg. I broke my leg when he went down. I'm helpless, Chet.'

'Throw down your rifle and I'll take a look at you,' Chet said.

Arnie looked as if he would ignore the order, but soon reached a decision. He tossed the rifle aside.

'If you're carrying other weapons then dump them now.'

Arnie produced a .45 pistol, and followed it with a smaller pocket gun. He raised his hands shoulder high and sat watching Chet with a defiant expression. Chet approached him and tossed the discarded weapons well out from Arnie's reach. He bent over the broken leg and examined it.

'This will need splinting before I can move you,' he said.

'There's a small ranch over yonder.' Arnie jerked a thumb. 'A man called Matt Sherman owns it. He's one of Frazee's men. Get him to bring his wagon here and pick me up. He'll take me into town to see the doc.'

'You were trailing Frazee. Where is he going?'

'I thought he was coming here, but his tracks turned off just short. I reckon he's heading for another county. He's got the bank dough, and he'll spend that before he gets another gang together and goes back into business.'

'I'll get him,' Chet said. 'His days are numbered. Tell me about my father. I reckon you know what happened to him, and if you do then spill it and I'll go easy on you.'

Arnie shook his head. 'See Sherman at the ranch, and tell him you're one of us. Take your law badge off. Play it as it comes. Do it now, and get a wagon here so I can get moving to town.'

Chet went back to his horse and mounted. He rode up a slope, and from the top he saw a ranch house in the distance, a single-storey building that looked more like a cabin. He removed his law star and dropped it into a pocket before continuing at a lope to the ranch. A man was standing in the front yard close to the door, holding a rifle. Chet rode up to him and reined in.

'I guess you're Matt Sherman,' he said.

'I am, and who are you?' Sherman was in his forties, tall and lean, his face weathered by his way of life. His eyes were brown, depthless, and showed suspicion as he studied Chet.

'I'm from Frazee,' Chet replied. 'I was coming here with Arnie Mayhew. His horse stepped into a hole, broke its leg, and Arnie broke his leg when the horse fell on him. He wants you to take a wagon to him and haul him into town to the doc.'

'I got better things to do,' Sherman grumbled.

'You're one of Frazee's gang, so you better do like you're told.'

'I'll do it if you stick around here until I get back,' Sherman replied. 'Come inside for a minute.'

Chet followed when Sherman turned abruptly, pushed open the door, and went into the building, which was bare of comfort and consisted of a single room. A rough wooden table stood in the centre of the room with several chairs around it, and a bunk was in a corner. There were no curtains at the two windows. A rack was nailed slightly lop-sided to an inner wall, and contained a selection of rifles and shotguns.

'I've been doing a special job for Frazee,' Sherman said. He pulled the heavy table out of position, pushed the chairs aside, and bent to lift a trapdoor, throwing it open with a resounding crash. A ladder of rough wood reached down into a storm cellar. Sherman drew his pistol and peered into the cellar. 'Hey, you down there, come on up and show yourself.'

Chet walked to Sherman's side and looked down into the darkness. A man ascended the ladder. He was old, around fifty, with grey hair showing at his temples. A battered Stetson topped a bearded face. He was wearing a dark blue town suit that was dirty, shabby. His hat shielded his face as he came out of the hole, and he staggered across to the table, pulled a chair up close, and sat down heavily. He was thin and unsteady, and sat gasping for air, his ribs heaving; chin down on his chest.

'Why are you holding him down there?' Chet demanded.

'It was Frazee's orders. The guy was the county sheriff until Frazee decided to replace him with two of the gang.'

Chet could not believe his ears. The world seemed to slip out of reality as his brain caught the import of what was said. He turned to Sherman as if in a dream, pulling his pistol from his waistband, swinging the weapon, smashing the barrel across Sherman's gun hand. Sherman yelled in pain and dropped his gun. He turned away, bellowing like an ox that had been hit in the neck with an axe. He dropped to his knees, grasping his injured hand.

'He's my father!' Chet said harshly. 'I was told he was dead, and you've been holding him down there like a wild animal.'

The old man looked up at Chet's words, straightened in his seat, gazing at Chet with disbelief in his eyes.

'Chet?' he said in a faltering tone. 'It is you, son! What in tarnation are you doing here?'

'It's a long story, Pa, and will have to wait.' Chet picked up Sherman's discarded gun and handed it to his father. 'Let me take care of Sherman before he starts getting ideas.'

'Put him down in the storm cellar,' Arch Hallam said. 'He won't get out of there in a hurry. I need to get back to town, Chet.'

'Hold your horses, Pa. I've been in the county a few days, and I've cleaned up some. I've got Arnie down on the ground just over the hill out front. He's got a broken leg.'

153

'It'll break your mother's heart when I arrest him,' Arch countered. 'He's been up to no good, but I'll get the deadwood on him and put him where he belongs. He's bad right through, Chet.'

'I've got enough evidence to put him away for a lifetime,' Chet replied. 'Save the talk until later, Pa. Mitch Frazee is loose around here somewhere, and I'd like to get him before he moves on to other parts.'

'What about his gang?'

'Arnie helped me get them earlier. There's only Frazee loose now.'

'You've done all this by yourself?'

'It happens like that sometimes. You'll see a lot of changes in town when you get back.' Chet paused and studied his father's gaunt face. 'I thought you were dead, Pa. I can't believe you're here.'

'There were times when I thought my last day had come, but I'm far from dead, son. I'll saddle a team to Sherman's wagon and we'll take him and Arnie into town. I need to get back to work.'

Chet nodded. 'There's a lot of law work to be done. I've just about filled the jail with prisoners, and they'll take a lot of sorting out. I'm a legal deputy.' He reached into his pocket, produced his badge, and pinned it to his shirt.

'I'll bet the bad men didn't know what hit them – an ex-Texas Ranger on the loose in Kansas.' The sheriff checked the pistol Chet had given him and then stood up. He pointed the weapon at Sherman, who was sitting on the floor holding his injured gun hand. 'Get up, Sherman,' he said. 'Get some rope,

154

Chet, and we'll hogtie him. Then we'll pick up Arnie and head for town.'

'Can you handle that chore alone? I'd like to get after Frazee while his trail is hot.'

'I've been sitting in that cellar for what seemed the biggest part of my life, and I'm raring to go. Just stick around until I've got Sherman helpless.'

Chet went to a window and looked out across the yard. Silence hung over the small spread. There was no movement anywhere. Arch took a lariat hanging from a nail by the gun rack and proceeded to tie Sherman, who complained about his hand.

'You stay here, Pa, and watch him,' Chet said. 'I'll get the wagon.'

'Your arm looks a mess. You'd better do the watching.'

'I'm not letting you out of my sight now I've found you,' Chet said firmly. 'I'll cover you. Frazee is around here, and I think he's wounded. I need to take him out.'

'We're two to his one,' Arch said, 'and I've got a big score to settle with him.'

Chet nodded and walked to the back door. He opened it a fraction and peered out, checking the backyard and a barn. There was no movement anywhere. He eased the door open wide and stepped outside, gun muzzle moving slowly.

'Don't come too close to me, Pa,' he said. 'Let's check out the barn. I can see a wagon over there beside it. I reckon the harness horses will be in the barn, huh?'

'You cover me while I check around,' Arch replied, and passed Chet and walked steadily towards the barn, his gun ready in his hand.

Chet was worried about his father. He moved out a little to his right, his left index finger tight against the trigger of his pistol. They reached the front of the barn without incident. The big door stood wide open. Arch pressed against the woodwork beside the aperture and eased forward, checking as he moved. He went into the barn and Chet moved into the doorway, covering the interior.

There was a line of stalls inside the barn. Three of them were occupied by horses. Arch stepped into the cover of a large grain bin, Chet moved forward and to the left of his father. He halted in the cover of a post holding up part of the roof. He was at the highest pitch of alertness, ears and eyes at work to detect the slightest unnatural sound or movement. A horse stamped, and his attention was drawn to the stalls.

Arch slid away from the grain bin and moved to check the horses. Chet remained motionless, his gun covering all directions. A few wisps of straw suddenly floated down from the loft above his head. He looked up and caught a glimpse through a narrow gap between two floorboards of a man moving stealthily above him. He yelled a warning to his father and tilted the muzzle of his gun upwards. Out of a corner of his eye he saw Arch disappearing through the doorway of a tack room.

At that moment a gun blasted the silence in the

barn and hurled a string of echoes across the ranch. Gun smoke flared overhead, and Chet saw splinters of wood leap from the doorway his father had passed through. He saw movement between two ill-fitting boards in the floor of the loft and triggered his gun three times, spacing his shots. He remained motionless until an uneasy silence returned, gun uplifted and watching for movement. But there was nothing.

'Are you OK, Chet?' Arch called tensely.

'Yeah, Pa. Stay where you are. The shot that almost got you came from up in the loft. I think I got him. I'll check out the loft.'

'I've got the loft covered, son,' Arch replied. 'Go ahead.'

Chet moved to the loft ladder and began to ascend. He had to use his right hand on the ladder, and the activity sent agonizing pain coursing through his arm. Step by step he climbed, and his head was just below the floor of the loft when Arch called to him.

'Hold it there, Chet.'

Chet paused, gun pointing upwards. He could feel sweat trickling down his face, soaking into his shirt. Arch's voice sounded again.

'Frazee, if you're up in the loft then throw down your gun and show yourself. You can't get away. There are two of us here, and half a dozen posse men around the place. You haven't got a chance. If you don't give up we'll fire the barn and shoot you when it gets too hot.'

'If you want me then come up and get me,' Frazee

157

shouted hoarsely. 'Stick up your head and I'll put a bullet through it.'

Chet took a fresh grip on the ladder and prepared to move on. The ladder slipped a fraction as he changed position, and Frazee triggered two shots. Chet ducked, and the ladder slid sideways. He yelled as he lost his grip and plunged to the ground, landing on his feet and sprawling sideways. His injured arm struck the ground when he rolled to absorb his impact, and he lost his grip on his pistol. He looked up at the loft, and saw Frazee peering down at him. Frazee pushed his pistol forward. Chet moved quickly, ignoring the pain in his arm. He looked for his gun but could not see it.

Arch fired two shots at Frazee, but the gang boss was already moving back without firing at Chet. Arch judged Frazee's position and fired another shot. Frazee yelled in sudden agony, and there was the sound of a body falling on the loft floor. Arch came forward, picked up the fallen ladder, and thrust it up into position. He started up the ladder, moving swiftly.

'Hold it, Pa,' Chet called. 'He might be luring you to go up. I don't want anything happening to you now. Keep the loft covered and I'll go up to it by the outside ladder.'

'I'll go,' Arch said instantly. 'It's about time I did something useful.'

'Stay where you are,' Chet said forcefully as he got to his feet, and Arch shook his head and moved back into a position of observation. 'Give me a couple of minutes, Pa,' he continued, 'and then fire some shots into this end of the loft to keep Frazee busy.'

Arch nodded. Chet got to his feet and looked around for his pistol. He found it, and checked the cylinder; fed fresh cartridges into the empty chambers, and left the barn. There was an exterior ladder giving access to the loft, and he went up it, gun ready in his left hand. He neared the top and paused, waiting for Arch to start shooting. When shots began to hammer inside the barn he sprang to the top of the ladder and lunged inside the loft.

He saw Frazee crouching at the far end of the loft, waiting in cover for the shooting by Arch to end. He dropped to his knees and raised his gun. Frazee heard him and turned like a cougar at bay, swinging his gun to fight it out. Chet dropped flat as he fired a single shot, and then rolled aside as Frazee's bullet pierced the top of his Stetson. He fired three shots, his foresight lined up on Frazee's chest. The barn shook to the thunder of the shooting. As Chet fired, he felt the lightning strike of a bullet passing through the top of his right shoulder. He saw Frazee through flaring gun smoke, and triggered his gun until the hammer clicked on an empty chamber.

Frazee fell sideways under the shock of striking lead, and fell out of the loft. Chet heard his father shouting that it was all over, and lost his senses. . . .

When he opened his eyes again there was silence in the barn, and the gun echoes had passed into the distance. He was lying on his back on the floor of the barn, and something had been wrapped around his

159

right shoulder to stanch the blood dribbling from his fresh wound. He heard feet on the loft ladder and felt around for his pistol, but Arch appeared before he could locate the weapon.

'So you're back with me, huh?' Arch said. 'Your shoulder ain't too bad. I've got the wagon ready for town and Arnie and Sherman are in it. They've got Frazee's body with them for company. Can you ride or shall I put you in the wagon?'

'I'll ride my horse,' Chet said, although his strength was at a low ebb. He grinned and began to push his body up from the boards. 'I reckon the shooting is about done now. But you've got a lot of paperwork to handle back in town, and a jail filled with prisoners who might be guilty of helping Frazee.'

'We'll worry about that when we get back to town,' said Arch, smiling. 'I owe you a vote of thanks, Chet, coming up from Texas to fight my battles.'

'I only did what a good son should do,' Chet replied. 'Come on, let's get back to town and put an end to Ma's uncertainty. She thinks you're dead.' He paused as a thought of Maisie slipped into his mind. 'I've got some unfinished business to deal with, Pa, and I ain't looking forward to it. I'd rather face a dozen men like Frazee than a woman like Maisie.'

'You got woman-trouble, son?' Arch shook his head. 'Now that is real bad trouble.'

They left the barn and set out for town, to face whatever lay waiting in the future. . . .

$\frac{u}{S}$ (H) ⌐ ·ꓤꓷ ꝑ